"Let me go, Clancy," Lisa said.

He shook his head. "You know I can't. If you want to get out of the house, I'll take you to the market tomorrow."

"You can't blame me for being restless under the circumstances," she said softly. "But the market will be fine."

"Have you been restless?" he murmured. "So have I. Do you suppose it springs from the same cause? If it does, I can suggest a better remedy than sightseeing." His hands reached up to cradle her face. Strong hands, yet they were a little unsteady as they touched her.

She excited him, and the knowledge increased her own arousal. She was trembling again. It seemed to be a permanent state when she was near Clancy.

"Not a safe remedy."

"I'd keep you safe. You'll always be safe with me." His thumbs rubbed gently at the corners of her mouth. "As safe as you want to be." His thumbs moved slowly to meet in the center of her lower lip. "Sometimes it can be fun to forget about safety. Haven't you found that?" He exerted the tiniest pressure and her lips parted. "I can feel the throbbing of your heart against my thumbs."

His dark head was lowering slowly. "Take a chance, Lisa," he urged. "Let me love you. . . ."

WHAT ARE *LOVESWEPT* ROMANCES?

They are stories of true romance and touching emotion. We believe those two very important ingredients are constants in our highly sensual and very believable stories in the LOVESWEPT line. Our goal is to give you, the reader, stories of consistently high quality that may sometimes make you laugh, sometimes make you cry, but are always fresh and creative and contain many delightful surprises within their pages.

Most romance fans read an enormous number of books. Those they truly love, they keep. Others may be traded with friends and soon forgotten. We hope that each *LOVESWEPT* romance will be a treasure—a "keeper." We will always try to publish

LOVE STORIES YOU'LL NEVER FORGET
BY AUTHORS YOU'LL ALWAYS REMEMBER

The Editors

LOVESWEPT® • 148

Iris Johansen
Always

BANTAM BOOKS
TORONTO • NEW YORK • LONDON • SYDNEY • AUCKLAND

ALWAYS

A Bantam Book / July 1986

ISBN 0-553-21749-6

Published simultaneously in the United States and Canada

PRINTED IN THE UNITED STATES OF AMERICA

O   0 9 8 7 6 5 4 3 2 1

One

Clancy Donahue leaned back in the plush visitor's chair and stretched his long legs out before him. "So she arrived four days ago in Paradise Cay," he commented. His eyes narrowed as Len Berthold nodded, then nervously shifted papers on the desk before him. "And what the hell's wrong with you, Len? You're acting skittish as the devil."

"I am skittish." Berthold grimaced. "I don't like being part of one of your games, Clancy. I'm an administrator now, out of the line of fire. I'd like it just fine if you set your little trap somewhere else."

"Too bad," Clancy said, and shrugged. "Your safe haven was the most convenient place to put the bait." His indolent position hadn't changed, but he was suddenly exuding a force that was almost tangible. "Paradise Cay is one of Sedikhan's possessions; this hotel casino is in Paradise Cay. I

1

made you manage here two years ago because you're tough, honest, and obey orders." His voice lowered to a silky murmur. "Do I have to tell you what would happen if I found you lacking in any of those qualities?"

Len moistened his lips. No, Donahue didn't have to tell him. It was all right there in the expression in those ice-blue eyes. He had known Donahue, security chief and right-hand man to Alex Ben Raschid, reigning head of Sedikhan, for over six years. Personally he had never run across a situation that didn't yield to the power Donahue wielded so effortlessly. But he had heard stories about the security chief's more direct methods, a number of which were violent and ruthless.

From the time word arrived that Donahue was flying in to handle personally the Landon matter, Len had known his comfortable berth here in Paradise Cay would probably heat up to a far from comfortable temperature. He cleared his throat. "It was just a comment, Clancy. You know I'll cooperate fully. I've obeyed your instructions to the letter. The Landon woman has been singing in the cafe since night before last." He frowned thoughtfully. "You know, she's not bad. She's got . . ." He hesitated as if searching for the appropriate word, then shrugged. "I don't know. Something."

"I'm not here to enjoy her singing talents," Clancy said a bit sarcastically. "Have you got Galbraith watching her?"

"Of course; I've had her under total surveillance since the moment she checked in." Berthold smiled faintly. "I haven't gotten that soft in the head since I left your service. She hasn't drawn a breath that we haven't known about. Baldwin definitely hasn't contacted her yet. I've also had a man calling the other hotels on the island every evening, and no man of his description has checked in."

Donahue frowned. "You're sure?"

"I'm sure. We circulated copies of that picture you sent, of course. He hasn't shown." Berthold brightened. "Maybe he's lost interest in the woman."

"No way. He'll show," Clancy said grimly. "Wherever Lisa Landon appears, he pops up like a jack-in-the-box. He's obsessed with her, and obsessions like that don't just lose their hold all of a sudden."

"But she divorced him over three years ago, according to what you told me," Berthold said. "Maybe he's finally taken the hint that he's not wanted."

Clancy shook his head. "She's an obsession," he repeated. "It's all in the dossier we've compiled on him: Jealous scenes, violence, even public threats. The works. He'll be here all right. He keeps a very close eye on the ex–Mrs. Baldwin. What time is she performing tonight?"

"The second show is at ten o'clock." Berthold glanced at the thin gold watch on his wrist. "That'll be about fifteen minutes from now. Do you want to watch it?"

Donahue nodded as he rose to his feet. "I'm going to talk to her tonight after the show to try to get her cooperation."

"And if not?"

"We'll use her anyway." His smile was a mere

baring of teeth. "I want that bastard Baldwin so bad I can taste it. Where's Galbraith now?"

"He should be in the cafe."

"Good." For a moment there was a thread of mischief in Clancy's smile. "Sorry to be a disgrace to your exclusive establishment, Len, but I won't have time to change. You'd better phone your headwaiter and tell him not to throw me out."

"I doubt if he'd try that." Berthold's glance traveled over Clancy's tall, massive build that did look as if it belonged more in a heavyweight boxing ring than an exclusive nightclub. Berthold remembered suddenly that Clancy had told him he had been a fighter once. But then Clancy had been something of a jack-of-all-trades before he became security chief of Sedikhan—and definitely master of the more lethal ones. "I will give Monty a ring, though, and tell him to extend all courtesies."

"Do that." Clancy turned to leave, moving with the lithe grace of absolute fitness and trained coordination. "I'm tired as hell and not in any mood for a hassle."

"Have you checked into the hotel or shall I do it for you?"

Clancy paused at the door. "I'll stay at my villa down the beach. It's close enough so that I can be on the spot in five minutes if I need to be. I'm tired of living in hotels. I've spent the last six weeks moving from city to city on Baldwin's trail." He took a key ring out of his pocket and tossed it across the room. It landed on the blotter in front of Berthold. "Send a maid down to open the villa for me right away, will you?" He didn't wait for an answer but shut the door behind him and set off briskly.

As he crossed the lushly carpeted foyer of the reception area, he made an effort to relax the tense muscles in his neck and shoulders. He hadn't lied when he'd told Len Berthold he was tired. He hadn't slept more than a few hours today on the long flight from Los Angeles to this tiny island in the Bahamas. L.A. had been a blind alley, too, dammit, he thought. Baldwin had gone underground without a ripple. Oh, well, if he couldn't find the rat's bolthole, he'd wait patiently until that rodent ventured out to nibble at his favorite delicacy, namely Lisa Landon.

The cafe was small and darkly intimate, like a thousand others he'd seen over the years. Postage-stamp-sized tables were covered with white damask cloths; candles in translucent cylinders cast half shadows over the faces of the guests speaking in quiet tones over drinks and hors d'oeuvres. A trio was playing soft, evocative jazz on the tiny stage at the far end of the room, and Clancy paused a moment in the doorway to listen. He'd always liked jazz. That fact had never failed to surprise Alex, and he could understand why. Jazz was the most lazily sensual and mellow music on the face of the earth, and laziness, mellowness, and sensuality were qualities that were absent in his personality. He was highly sexed and required women fairly frequently, but it was always just a hunger to be appeased and then forgotten. Sensuality required softer, gentler emotions, the kind his profession had allowed little time to cultivate. Still, he did like jazz, and this trio was surprisingly good.

"Clancy?"

His head swiveled quickly to the left. Galbraith.

"John." Clancy nodded in acknowledgment to the man standing close to him. Galbraith was dressed in impeccable evening clothes and blended into his elegant surroundings with the adaptability of a chameleon. His features were handsome, but not too handsome. His brown hair was cut in a trendy but not avant-garde style, and his smile was as deceptively cheerful and wholesome as a college boy's. Not that college kids were more wholesome than anyone else these days, Clancy thought wearily. Childhood didn't last much past puberty in a world as crisis-shadowed as this one. "Do you have a table?"

Galbraith gestured. "Ringside. I usually sit toward the back when I'm doing surveillance, but I thought you'd prefer to have a closer look at her. You said on the phone that you were going to talk to her, anyway." He turned and led the way through the thickly clustered tables. He dropped into a chair at the ringside table he'd indicated and picked up a half-empty highball glass. His eyes, set deep in his round, tanned face, were as bright and inquisitive as a squirrel's. "You look really beat, Clancy. What the hell have you been doing to yourself?"

"The usual." Clancy sat down and shook his head at the waiter who paused to look at him inquiringly. He wanted to keep a clear head, and he was too tired to risk even the slightest alcohol haze. "No sign of Baldwin?"

"Not one. She's made no telephone calls since she's been here. She takes long walks on the beach every day, but she doesn't speak to anyone." He shrugged. "Or no one important. She stopped this afternoon and helped a little kid build a sand castle. Then she came back to the hotel, rehearsed with the trio, and had dinner in her room. She does two shows a night here and then goes back to her room. No men since she's arrived on the island."

"Not off the island, either," Clancy said slowly. "Odd. It could mean she's still carrying a torch for Baldwin." His lips twisted. "Or maybe she's frigid and that's the challenge she poses for him."

"No," Galbraith said quickly and with utmost certainty. Then, as Clancy looked at him in surprise, he muttered sheepishly, "I mean, I can't imagine her being cold to anyone she cared about."

"She seems to have impressed you," Clancy said. "Is the lady that much of a femme fatale?"

Galbraith shifted uncomfortably. "No. Hell, you know I've never had a thing for older women."

"And she's all of thirty-seven. Practically ancient," Clancy said dryly. "She must be very beautiful to make you overlook her rapidly advancing decrepitude."

"No." Galbraith was frowning abstractedly and Clancy doubted if he even caught the sarcasm. "At least, I don't think she is. It's hard to tell." He made a little gesture with one hand. "She's just got something. . . ."

"That's what Berthold said." Clancy smiled faintly. "I'm beginning to be a bit curious about this singer who makes tough bastards like the two of you inarticulate. Does this phenomenon have a decent voice, or shall I put on my ear plugs?"

"She's damn good," Galbraith said. "Too good

for a place like this. She reminds me a little of Streisand."

Clancy lifted a brow. "Praise indeed. I can hardly wait to hear the lady and formulate my own definition of that special 'something' you think she has."

"Well, you won't have to wait long." Galbraith nodded at the pianist, who had pulled a stool in front of the microphone and was carefully adjusting it. "She's on right now."

The introduction by the pianist was straightforward and without fanfare, and so was the woman who walked gracefully to the microphone and sat down on the stool. She was dressed in an elegantly tailored, long-sleeved white silk blouse and an ankle-length black evening skirt that had a vaguely Edwardian air except for the long center slit that reached midthigh. She was tall, Clancy noticed, and gracefully fine-boned instead of sexy as he had expected. Her long hair was a shade somewhere between light brown and honey and was drawn cleanly away from her face and fastened in back with a barrette. It was difficult to make out her features in the dimness of the cafe, but they didn't appear exceptionally attractive. Then the spotlight came on.

Warmth. Gentle warmth in wide-set brown eyes. Her face held a touch of sadness in repose, but then she smiled. Sensitive, beautifully shaped lips smiled suddenly at the audience with such loving kindness that it made Clancy feel oddly breathless. "Hello, I'm Lisa. I have a few songs I'm going to sing for you tonight." She spoke with a casual intimacy as if to a room filled with old friends. "Then I'm going to take requests." She made a face. "Please, no opera. Madame Butterfly I'm not." She chuckled in delight as she heard the whisper of laughter around the room, and Clancy felt again a queer half-aching tug at his emotions. What the hell was happening to him? "Ready?" She nodded at the pianist, who started the introduction. "Here we go."

During the next forty-five minutes Clancy realized that Galbraith and Berthold were right: Lisa Landon *was* good. Her clear, bell-like notes held a hint of power skillfully restrained, and the emotion she conveyed was amazing. But he could scarcely appreciate her talent because his attention was focused on the woman, not the singer. The nervous, graceful hands that moved in impulsive gestures. The line of her creamy throat that rose from the stark white of her blouse. What a beautiful throat. Camellia soft, yet breathing, pulsing with life as no flower ever could. And that smile . . . His lips curved in a self-mocking grin as he realized how poetic he was waxing. When aroused he was usually more interested in breasts and hips than throats and smiles. And there was no question that he was aroused now. There was an aching in his groin that was bewildering in its intensity and filled him with a faint sense of anger. It was a totally illogical reaction. The woman wasn't even that attractive. She was too thin and her mouth was a little large. Her legs were lovely, he admitted grudgingly, and heaven only knew that she was showing enough of them in that slit skirt.

Possessiveness. Damn, the emotion had slipped into his thoughts without his even being aware of it. When had he ever felt possessive about any woman? And this woman was a complete stranger.

The round of requests had ended now and Lisa Landon slipped from the stool and smiled again. Then she was gone from the stage as quickly as she had come.

Galbraith leaned forward and grinned at Clancy. "Well, have you defined the 'something' the lady's got?"

Me. She's got me. The answer emerged swiftly and instinctively from the jumble of emotions that was whirling within Clancy. He rejected the thought as quickly as it came. "Character," he said lightly. "And maturity. I can see how a boy like you would be dazzled by those qualities. The pretty dolls I've seen you squiring around have a few years to go before they begin acquiring them."

"The pretty dolls are entertaining," Galbraith drawled. "And I think that old poker face of yours slipped enough so that I could see you were dazzled by the qualities of the lady."

"You're getting fresh, John." Clancy pushed back his chair and rose to his feet. "Remind me to slap you down the next time you annoy me. It will do wonders for your own character development."

Galbraith grimaced. "I won't have to remind you. You remember everything. Unfortunately. I suppose you're going backstage. Do you want me to wait and continue surveillance?"

Clancy hesitated. "No," he said slowly. "I'll take care of it."

Galbraith's brows lifted in surprise. "Really? It must be years since you did any chore as plebeian as surveillance. Are you sure you remember how?"

"Fresh." Clancy enunciated the word distinctly. "Very fresh. I assure you I'll muddle through."

Galbraith's cheeky grin faded as he silently cursed himself. It wasn't safe to bait Clancy who, when he lost patience, could turn and mete out punishment efficiently. Galbraith held up his hands. "Joking." He smiled. "I'm no fool, Clancy. I know what you are."

"It's nice that you're so confident of your perceptiveness," Clancy said with a slightly enigmatic smile. "There are times when I'm not at all sure that I know." He turned and walked swiftly across the tiny dance floor to the arched doorway through which Lisa Landon had disappeared.

The knock on the dressing room door was brisk and authoritative.

Lisa tensed, then consciously forced herself to relax. It couldn't be he. She'd seen no sign of Martin since she'd arrived here. She mustn't let her imagination run wild just because a knock on the door was demanding instead of politely perfunctory. She reached for a tissue and began wiping the cream from her face. "Come in."

"For God's sake, didn't anyone ever tell you that you don't leave your door unlocked and invite just anyone who's on the other side to come in?" The man who stood in the doorway was frowning and his voice was harsh. "For all you knew, I could have been Jack the Ripper."

Her eyes widened in surprise as she turned away from the mirror to look at him. "You're not Jack the Ripper," she muttered. The man did look dangerous though. He stood well over six feet with the broad shoulders and the deep chest of a longshoreman. His features were rough and craggy, with broad cheekbones and a nose that had been broken at some time or other. He had the golden tan of a man who lived in the hot sun of the tropics, and his hair might once have been raven dark but was now flecked with silver. He gave the impression of a man fully mature, fully in control, and very used to having his own way. She found herself instinctively rebelling against him. She'd had her fill of men who wanted their own way. She lifted her chin. "It's true you could be just as disreputable as Jack the Ripper. So perhaps you should leave."

His expression didn't change, but she had the impression she'd surprised him. Suddenly he smiled with a beguiling warmth. The transformation of his rough-hewn face gave her a little shock.

"I was rude, wasn't I? You'll have to forgive me." There was the faintest trace of a brogue in his deep voice. "I've always been too blunt. It's one of my greatest faults. My name is Clancy Donahue, Miss Landon. I'd like to talk to you, if I may." His blue eyes were suddenly twinkling. "I'll let you search me if it will make you feel any safer. I'm totally without weapons of any sort."

She doubted that. There was nothing in the least defenseless about Clancy Donahue. His wickedly appealing smile caused her to smile in return. "I'll trust you. Come in, Mr. Donahue. What can I do for you?" She resumed wiping the cream from her face.

He closed the door and the size of the dressing room seemed to shrink. "I want your cooperation."

He came forward to stand before her. "You've missed a spot. Here, let me." He took the tissue and carefully wiped the blob of cream from her temple. For someone with such large hands, he was very gentle. It was an intimate gesture performed with surprising matter-of-factness. "There. That does it." He tossed the tissue on the vanity. "I like you better without makeup. Your skin is really quite extraordinary." He spoke almost abstractedly. "So white and soft. Like a camellia. I was thinking that while I was watching you sing tonight."

"You were in the audience?" She couldn't hide her surprise as she glanced at his casual jeans and navy crew-neck sweater. She had known the head-waiter for only a few days, but she was aware that Monty was snobbish and rigid about his precious dress code.

Clancy's lips twisted. "I have friends in high places."

"You must." Lisa wished he'd move away from her. She could feel the heat emanating from his big body even though he was no longer touching her, and she was conscious of the clean scent of soap and an after-shave that smelled vaguely minty. She'd been shockingly aware of the physical presence of the man since he'd walked in the door, and she wasn't sure she liked having her composure disturbed. She had fought too long and too hard to gain that composure. Nodding, she gestured to the chair across the room. "Won't you sit down?" He moved away at once and she let her breath out in a little rush. How stupid to feel threatened because he was a virile male and she was merely experiencing a very natural sexual chemistry. "You said something about cooperation?"

He dropped into the chair she'd indicated. "In my search for Martin Baldwin," he said bluntly. "I think you can deliver him to me."

She stiffened. "You're a policeman?"

He shook his head. "I'm with the Sedikhan Security Service. Your ex-husband and his 'company' have been running guns to a group of terrorists based across the border from Sedikhan in Said Ababa." His expression hardened. "I don't like men who make money off of that terror any more than I like the terrorists themselves. I want very much to find Baldwin."

Lisa moistened her lips. Oh, dear Lord, would it never end? "Then go find him," she said quietly. "It has nothing to do with me."

"I need you. Baldwin knows I'm looking for him and has gone underground. The only person who can make him come out of hiding is you."

She lowered her lashes to veil her eyes. "We're not married any longer. I have nothing to do with Martin these days."

"Not willingly, perhaps." Clancy shrugged. "But he still wants you. Would you like me to quote a few instances of Baldwin's pathological jealousy? You lost a very good job in Las Vegas because Baldwin made a scene and threatened to cut a customer's throat. That was about a year ago, wasn't it? There have been two other ugly scenes since that I can think of offhand. I have the dossier in my suitcase if you'd like to review it."

"No," she said numbly. Of course he would have a dossier on her. All policemen had their damned dossiers. She should know that by now. "I just want to be left alone. I'm not involved in Martin's activities. I never have been."

"I know," he said in a gentle tone. "But you'll remain involved as long as he's in your life. Give him to me and I'll promise to remove him." He paused deliberately. "Permanently."

Her gaze lifted swiftly to his. She smiled with an effort. "You sound quite lethal. The last I heard, gun running wasn't a capital offense."

"Perhaps not in the U.S., but in Sedikhan it's a different situation entirely." He smiled with a touch of cold ferocity. "Alex leaves judgments of that nature up to me."

"Alex?"

"Alex Ben Raschid, the sheikh of Sedikhan. Alex is a very busy man these days. I assure you I have full power to act for him. Is it a deal?"

"You'd kill him?" Lisa whispered.

"Perhaps; I haven't decided as yet. In any event, he won't be around to bother you again. Isn't that what you want?"

She shivered. "Not that way. I could never be that cold-blooded."

His lips tightened. "Baldwin is a hell of a lot more cold-blooded than you could ever dream of being. What kind of man do you think would furnish hand grenades and dynamite to terrorists when he knows damn well they'll be used to blow up schoolbuses and supermarkets? Two children were killed last year in Marasef and several more were injured. I can't touch the terrorists as long as Said Ababa is protecting them, but I can stop their flow of weapons." He paused. "I can stop Baldwin."

"Children were hurt?" She felt suddenly sick. How could Martin do these things? It was unbelievable.

Clancy nodded curtly. "Will you help me?"

She drew a deep breath. "I can't."

"You can. But you won't. Perhaps you're one of those women who get some sort of kinky thrill out of being desired by a bastard like that. Maybe it's a little game the two of you play."

"A game!" Her brown eyes were blazing. "Do you think I enjoy having my career slowly destroyed in the most humiliating way possible? That I like being afraid every time I hear a knock on the door that it will be him and the whole sordid mess will start again? You're a very stupid man, Mr. Donahue."

"Then give him to me," Clancy said relentlessly. "Cooperate."

"I can't, dammit." She jumped to her feet. "He was my husband. I had his child. It doesn't matter what he did. I can't be your Judas goat. Not and still live with myself."

"Child?" Clancy repeated slowly.

She could feel the blood drain from her face. Don't think about it; keep the pain at bay, she silently commanded herself. "Didn't your neat little reports mention that?" she asked bitterly. "Perhaps your informants didn't consider the birth of my little boy important. It wasn't exactly a world-shaking event." Her voice dropped to a husky whisper. "Except to me."

"I'm sure it must have been in the report. I must have overlooked it." Clancy found his hands unconsciously tightening on the arms of the chair.

The idea of her bearing that bastard's child filled him with a totally irrational rage.

"How careless of you." She wouldn't cry. Oh, God, she had thought all the tears had been shed long ago. Why were her eyes stinging with them now? Firmly she blinked the moisture away and lifted her chin. "But you can see that I wouldn't be able to do as you ask."

"You refuse?"

She nodded. "I'm sorry, but you'll have to catch Martin on your own. You'll get no help from me."

"I'm sorry too." A fleeting expression of regret was replaced by a look of fierce determination. "I wanted your cooperation. I don't like using force unless it's absolutely necessary."

"Force!" Her eyes widened with disbelief. "How could you possibly force me?"

"Very painlessly, I hope. Once you realize that I hold all the cards, I think you'll be sensible." He sat forward. "Let me tell you exactly what you're going to do. You'll continue to sing here until Baldwin shows up." His lips twisted. "And we both know he'll do so eventually. It's obvious that I can't convince you to tip my man when you see him, but you're not to blow our surveillance to Baldwin, either. Once he's spotted, we'll move in and take over."

She shook her head as if to clear it. "Didn't you hear me? I won't help you. Not actively nor passively. If you expect Martin to show up here, then I'll leave. I have only two more nights to this engagement anyway."

"Wrong," he said succinctly. "I didn't bring you here to let you go before you served my purpose.

You're the bait that's going to lure my rat out of the woodwork."

"You didn't bring . . ." Understanding suddenly dawned. "*You* arranged for me to come here to Paradise Cay? What do you have to do with this place?"

He shrugged. "The island is a Sedikhan possession and so is most of the real estate on it. That's not widely known since Alex purchased it only two years ago, so Baldwin shouldn't learn that you're sitting squarely in the lion's mouth until it snaps shut."

"Charming," she said. "I suppose I should have suspected something. The deal was much too generous for a singer who is still struggling on the bottom rungs of the ladder." She laughed mirthlessly. "I was very excited about it, you know. I thought I was getting somewhere at last."

"You'll get there. You're extraordinarily talented. After your stint here, I'll arrange for you to meet a few people who'll be glad to help." He smiled grimly. "I'll just call in a few debts."

"Bribery?" She felt the color rush to her cheeks. "Just close my eyes and be rewarded with a payoff? No, thank you, Mr. Donahue."

"I didn't mean it like that," he snapped. "I just wanted to help."

"Well, I don't want to help you," she said hotly. "And I'm not about to. Tomorrow I'll take the first flight back to Miami. This engagement is now officially at an end."

"That's your last word on it?" Clancy asked calmly.

She nodded. "I won't be used by you. I won't be used by anyone, dammit."

He stood up. "You will, you know. I'll just have to find another trap to bait." He turned and walked toward the door. "Good night, Miss Landon."

Her hands clenched at her sides. "He may not even come," she burst out in exasperation.

He opened the door. "You underestimate yourself. Baldwin will come." He paused, and for an instant something flickered in his eyes that sent a tremor through her. "I would." He softly closed the door behind him.

When Clancy left the dressing room he proceeded directly to his villa. He dialed Alex's private number as soon as he reached the study. It was answered almost at once, as he'd thought it would be. Since the terrorist situation had taken on such dangerous proportions in Sedikhan, Alex often burned the midnight oil.

"Alex? I may need you to pull some diplomatic strings in the U.S. I'll try to cover myself as much as possible, but it may get a bit dicey."

"Baldwin?" Alex asked. "That shouldn't be too difficult. He has both drug smuggling and assault with intent to kill charges pending against him in Miami."

"Not Baldwin." Clancy hesitated. "His ex-wife. I'm going to kidnap her."

There was a long silence on the other end of the line. "Kidnap an American citizen? I can see how that could get a little dicey. You're sure it's necessary?"

"It's necessary," Clancy said. "I just thought I'd warn you in case I have to send out a Mayday."

"Is she collaborating with Baldwin?"

"No, of course not. She wouldn't—" He broke off. He sounded as defensive as Galbraith had earlier, he realized with exasperation. He finished lamely, "She's not involved."

"Oh, you're going to kidnap an *innocent* American citizen." Suddenly Alex chuckled. "Why do I have the feeling that you've stumbled across something that you can't handle?"

"I can handle it."

"I sincerely hope so," Alex drawled. "You wouldn't consider giving up your little captive in the interest of diplomacy?"

"I would not."

"I didn't think so." Alex's tone was slightly whimsical. "All right, Clancy. Make off with your little houri. I'll take the flak if it comes down to it. Enjoy."

"Enjoy!" Clancy said. "Dammit, this is business . . . your business."

"Is it?" Alex murmured softly. "Somehow I have my doubts about that. If I can help, let me know. If I'd found it necessary with Sabrina, I would probably have done the same thing. Keep in touch." The dial tone sounded as Alex hung up.

Clancy slowly replaced the receiver. Damn Alex, anyway. They were so close that it had always been impossible to deceive him even if he succeeded in deceiving himself.

Alex was right. His primary reason for keeping Lisa Landon on Paradise Cay had altered drastically in the brief time in her dressing room. Yet how could he explain to Alex what he didn't understand himself? His responses had always been firmly under his control until that spotlight had suddenly highlighted Lisa Landon's serene figure sitting on the tiny stage. Now he didn't know how to sort out what he was feeling. Admiration for her integrity mixed with sympathy, jealousy, possessiveness, desire—and anger at her ability to arouse and confuse him to this extent.

He had never lied to himself, and he wasn't about to start now. Even if Lisa hadn't been the key to capturing Baldwin, he would still have found a way to see that she stayed here. What was he thinking? He'd been exposed to Alex's Eastern temperament too long. He wasn't an impulsive boy like Galbraith; he was a mature man. He couldn't just grab a woman and expect her not to cause an uproar. He would have to be gentle and patient and let her become accustomed to the idea that she belonged— He was doing it again, dammit. She didn't belong to him. She was an independent woman.

He strolled restlessly to the French doors and out into the courtyard. The night air was soft and fragrant with hibiscus and honeysuckle. Would she like it here? She was rather like a flower herself— soft and fragrant, yet with a quiet strength that revealed her sturdy roots. He would like to see her in this serene oasis with its mosaic fountain and flowering shrubs . . . or better still, in his garden at home in Marasef. He shook his head ruefully. Now he sounded like his old friend David Bradford, with his gardener's passion for flowers. This was evidently his night for behaving out of character.

He was a man of action, not a poet or a gardener. He straightened his shoulders and turned back to the house.

And now it was time for him to do what he did best. Lisa had said she was leaving in the morning, and that meant there wasn't much time to accomplish his purpose. He'd have to phone Galbraith and Berthold and give orders and instructions. There'd be no trouble with Galbraith, but Berthold might balk. He showed definite signs of becoming a problem. The easy life did that to some people. Clancy's pace quickened with brisk determination as he entered the library. His former weariness was forgotten as he headed for the phone on the desk. There wasn't time to indulge himself to that extent. He had a kidnapping to arrange.

Two

The warm night air was like a gentle caress against her cheek, and the moonlight silvered the dark waters of the surf beneath her balcony with an exquisite radiance. It was winter in New York now, Lisa remembered with a shiver. She had always hated winter. What would it be like to live forever on an island where winter never came? Wearily she brushed back a lock of hair from her temple. She would never know, and it was foolishly fanciful even to wonder. Singing engagements on tropical islands came very rarely. She had been elated when her agent had told her about the offer of this job on Paradise Cay, and she'd jumped at the chance to get away from the snows and slush of New York.

Well, it was obvious she had jumped too readily at the carrot Clancy Donahue had dangled before her. Martin again. Would she never be free of him?

Sometimes she felt he would always be there, casting a dark shadow, igniting memories of Tommy—No, she mustn't think. As long as she didn't think, that part of her remained frozen and blessedly painless. She had fought hard to gain that shield of ice, that forgetfulness. If she'd been forced to yield laughter and a zest for life in exchange, she still regarded it as a fair trade.

The phone rang and she started in surprise. It was after midnight and she knew no one who would call at this hour.

Except Martin.

For the past three years, Martin had called her at all hours of the day or night from whatever part of the world he happened to be in. It had done no good to change her telephone number; he always found out the new one eventually. She wouldn't answer it at all, she thought with swift panic. But she knew she would. She always did. She turned and strode swiftly to the bedside table in her room and picked up the receiver. "Hello."

"Are you all right?" Clancy Donahue's tone was harsh. "For heaven's sake, the phone nearly rang off the hook."

She felt limp with relief and sank down on the bed. "Of course I'm all right." She drew a deep breath and tried to steady her heartbeat. "It's after midnight. Didn't it occur to you that I might be sleeping?"

"Were you?"

She didn't answer the question. "Why are you calling, Mr. Donahue? I thought we had said all there was to say."

There was a short silence. "I decided to give you a

chance to change your mind," he said finally. "Will you help us?"

"No, I will not," she said. "You don't seem to be able to understand a refusal, Mr. Donahue. My bags are packed and I have reservations on the eight o'clock flight to Miami. You can look elsewhere for bait for your trap."

"You're the only bait Baldwin finds appetizing," he said tersely. "You're quite sure?"

She sighed. "I'm quite sure. Give up, Mr. Donahue."

"Why? The battle has just begun." His voice lowered. "I'm sorry. Believe me, I didn't want it this way."

He rang off before she could reply, and a faint frown knotted her brow as she slowly replaced the receiver. Donahue's last remark had filled her with uneasiness. The man himself made her uneasy. He was one of those bigger-than-life figures one ran into—thankfully—with great rarity. He was too much of everything for her to feel comfortable. Too intelligent, too confident, too virile. He emitted an aura of power that disturbed her. It was just as well she was leaving tomorrow. Nothing must be allowed to break through the wall that surrounded her emotions, and she had an idea that Clancy Donahue didn't believe there was a wall in existence that he couldn't burst through. Yes, it was just as well she wouldn't see him again.

Lisa stood up and strode into the bathroom. She opened a small plastic container, took out two sleeping pills, and swallowed them quickly. Although she had been cutting down on the medication for the last two months, she knew she was too upset to sleep dreamlessly tonight. And the dreams must *not* come. Not again. She set her travel alarm, took off her robe, and slipped between the sheets. Then she reached over to flick off the light and settled back against the pillows. Closing her eyes, she breathed deeply and tried to relax every muscle and empty her mind of everything. She felt a tiny flutter of panic in the pit of her stomach and crushed it down swiftly. There was no reason to be frightened. The sleeping pills would take hold soon and there would be no dreams. No dreams at all. . . .

There were dreams, but they weren't the heavy, somber nightmares that she had dreaded. These were strangely disjointed fragments, a sharp prick on her arm, masculine voices, lights, and then the dreams were lost in shifting darkness that billowed and flowed with moments of misty clarity.

"Dammit, she's unconscious. That drug was only a mild sedative. It shouldn't have knocked her out. How the hell much did you give her?" Clancy Donahue's rough voice. She supposed it wasn't all that unusual. One of the last things on her mind before she had gone to sleep had been Donahue, but she wished he wouldn't sound so angry.

"I gave her the dosage you told me." A younger voice . . . definitely defensive. "How did I know she was on sleeping pills? We found these in the bathroom, when we couldn't wake her up."

"Damn, this prescription is potent. I don't even know if the drugs are dangerous to mix. I'll have to call the lab in Sedikhan. Watch her closely. If there's any sign of respiratory failure or deepening unconsciousness, call me on the double."

The darkness deepened again. She was being carried. Mint. Donahue. The same after-shave she had noticed earlier in her dressing room. It was fresh and pleasant, just as the arms that were holding her were pleasant. Warm and strong and as gentle as his voice was harsh. She made a contented sound deep in her throat that was almost a purr and nestled her cheek closer against that hard, muscular chest. How wonderful to relax and be held so protectively. Surely arms this strong c uld keep away the dreams. "Safe." The word was only a whisper.

The arms tightened around her. "That's right." Donahue's voice was no longer harsh, but velvet soft. "You're safe, Lisa. I'll keep you safe from now on."

It wasn't true. No one could keep her safe from the dreams. Yet it was nice to pretend for a little while. "Thank you," she murmured drowsily.

His chuckle was a bit husky as it reverberated beneath her ear. "I doubt if you'll be quite as grateful to me when you regain consciousness." She was being placed on something soft and cushioned, and the arms were suddenly gone. She muttered a protest. "It's all right, I'm still here." The mattress sank beneath his weight, and he gathered her hands in his warm clasp. "I'll be here when you wake up. I won't let you go." One hand loosened its clasp to brush an errant tress back from her forehead and then began to stroke the hair at her temple. "Go to sleep."

"You'll keep the dreams away?"

His hand halted its motion for the briefest instant before resuming the stroking. "If that's what you want."

"Oh, yes, please," she whispered. "That's what I want."

"Then I'll keep the dreams away. Go to sleep, Lisa. I won't let the dreams come back."

She could almost believe him. She let the resistance flow out of her and the darkness take her.

She was asleep. Carefully Clancy released Lisa's hands and stood up. According to what the lab had told him, she would be unconscious for at least ten to twelve hours; yet he was reluctant to leave her. She looked so damned *alone*. Her honey-beige hair, fanned out on the white pillow, was as tumbled and silky as a small child's. Her lips were pink and crumpled, slightly parted with the deepness of her breathing. She was probably no longer aware that he was with her, but somehow it made no difference. He had promised that he would protect her, that he would keep away the dreams she feared so much. What nightmares could be so terrible that fear of them would pierce a drug-induced sleep as deep as Lisa's? He had a sudden irresistible compulsion to *know*.

He strode to the door and grabbed his suitcase, which he hadn't yet bothered to unpack. Setting it down on the low padded bench at the foot of the king-sized bed, he unsnapped it and threw open the lid. The dossier on Lisa Landon was on top. He'd scanned it briefly before boarding the plane in L.A., planning to go through it thoroughly later. At the time he'd been more interested in Baldwin's relationship with his ex-wife than in any more personal details. Now he wanted to know everything about the woman curled up on his bed like a bereft child. He dragged the cane chair across the room and settled himself as comfortably as possible. The chair wasn't built for a man of his size, he thought wearily. It was going to be as uncomfortable as the devil by the time Lisa woke up. Well, he'd been a hell of a lot more uncomfortable any number of times in his life for less reason. He slipped off his shoes and propped his feet on the bed. Then he opened the manila folder and began to read about Lisa Landon.

One moment Lisa was sleeping deeply and the next she was wide awake. Ice-blue eyes were narrowed on her face. Clancy Donahue's eyes. But what was he doing in her room? "What are you . . ." She sat up straight in the bed and then wished she hadn't moved so quickly as the room whirled in dark, sweeping circles around her.

She heard a muttered curse from Donahue. Then he was sitting beside her on the bed, his hands cupping her shoulders, steadying her. "Easy. Do you always wake up this abruptly?"

"No. Yes." Her head was muzzy and she shook it, but she still couldn't seem to think straight. "I don't know." She did know, however, that something was very wrong about Clancy Donahue being here in her room. Her tongue felt coated and her words were slightly slurred. "You shouldn't . . ."

"Lie down." He pushed her back on the pillow. "Give yourself time to wake up and come to terms with the situation before you decide to take me on." He smiled grimly. "I'm sure that time will come soon enough."

"What are you doing in my room?" But it wasn't her room! she suddenly realized. The bed she was lying on was king-, not queen-sized, the spread dark blue, not charcoal-and-yellow stripes, the walls beige, not pale gray. She was still wearing the same tailored white satin pajamas, but everything else was wildly, terribly wrong. Her eyes widened with shock and she tried to sit up again.

The movement was immediately frustrated by Donahue's hands on her shoulders pressing her back down. "No, it's not your room," he said quietly. "You're no longer at the hotel. This is my bedroom at a villa located about a half mile from the casino. There's no reason to be afraid. You're perfectly safe and will remain so. I promise you."

"Your bedroom?" Lisa stared at him in stunned disbelief. "What am I doing . . ." She stopped as she remembered the disjointed half dreams that had plagued her sleep. "You kidnapped me," she whispered. She couldn't believe it. "You actually kidnapped me?"

He nodded. "It was necessary," he said simply. "I have to get Baldwin. I told you that."

"So you kidnapped me," she said. "Another trap, you said. I wouldn't act as bait in the trap, so you just moved the bait to another trap." She raised her hand and pushed the hair away from her forehead. "Is that what you did?"

"That's what I did. I told you I wanted your cooperation. I'm sorry it had to be this way."

"Sorry!" The anger was curling through her veins, burning away the haze that had befuddled her senses. "Dammit, you kidnapped me and all you can say is that you're *sorry*? You committed a crime!"

"Yes, I know." Clancy frowned. "I wish you'd try to go back to sleep. We can discuss this later. According to the doctors, you should have slept another five hours. I'm not sure this upset is good for you."

"You don't think it's normal for me to be upset about being kidnapped? It may be commonplace in your life-style, but it's not in mine." Her eyes were blazing up at him. "I've never been kidnapped before."

His lips tightened. "I don't go around kidnapping people off the streets, Miss Landon."

"No? Should I be flattered that you selected me?" She struggled to a sitting position, throwing off his hands. "Well, I'm not, Mr. Donahue. I'm mad as hell."

"I can see that," he said dryly. "I didn't expect anything else. However, I'm afraid you'll have to resign yourself to the fact and make yourself as comfortable as possible. You're here, and you'll remain here until Baldwin shows up."

"The hell I will." She leaped out of bed and started to run toward the door. But there was something wrong with her legs. They felt weak and flaccid, and her head was whirling again. There was a sudden sharp pain as she stumbled blindly and fell to her knees on the carpet.

Vaguely Lisa heard Donahue's low curse, and then he was on his knees beside her. "What the hell do you think you're doing?" His arms were about her, her face crushed against his chest. Mint and soap and musk again, she thought dully. "I told you that you should stay in bed. You had a drug overdose. How the hell do you expect to go running around when you can hardly hold your head up?"

"I wasn't running around. I was escaping," she muttered. Even through the whirling darkness it seemed important that the distinction be made. Desperately she clutched his sweater to try and steady herself. "Drugs?"

"We gave you a harmless sedative. We had no idea that you took sleeping pills." His arms tightened around her. "You shouldn't take the damn things, anyway. Why the hell do you?"

"I need them." The darkness was clearing again. She tried to raise her head from his chest, but discovered it felt far too heavy. "Besides, it's none of your business."

"Isn't it?" It was almost a growl. "The hell it's not." He was suddenly on his feet, pulling her with him. "*You're* my business from now on." He lifted her up and carried her to the bed. "I think it's about time you were someone's concern. You sure as hell don't seem to be able to take care of yourself."

She knew she should resent that slur on her independence. And she would—as soon as she could muster enough strength to feel anything at all. "I need the sleeping pills," she whispered again. It seemed important that he realize that.

"Not anymore." There was a thread of grimness in his voice. "We'll find a substitute." He placed her on the bed and covered her carefully with the sheet. "Now listen to me. Okay?" His expression was as grim as his voice had been. "I know you're angry, and you have a perfect right to be. I'd feel the same way, but angry or not, the situation exists. You'll either be a guest or a prisoner. The choice is entirely your own. This place is located on a stretch of private beach, and you can scream the house down and no one will hear you. There will be two men on duty at both front and back entrances at all times. If you manage to knock me out or cut my throat, as I'm sure you're tempted to do, you'll still have them to contend with." He sat back down on the chair by the bed. "Here's the way we play it. The hotel staff has been given the story that you left your singing engagement so abruptly because you've made a connection with a wealthy American oilman, Paul Desmond." He indicated himself with a half-mocking gesture. "You've moved into a love nest down the beach and will soon be returning with him to Texas. That should bring Baldwin running."

"No. . . ."

"I take it that's a protest, not disagreement. We both know he'll come, Lisa. He has a history of psychotic jealousy where you're concerned."

She was having trouble keeping her lids from closing. "I won't let you do this," she murmured. "I'm going to get away." Her eyes closed in spite of her struggle to keep them open. "I'm going to get away from you, Donahue."

Was it her imagination or did she feel a whisper-soft caress as he brushed a curl away from her temple? "It's too late, Lisa." The words came out of the hovering darkness, blurred but unmistakable. "You'll never get away from me."

* * *

When she opened her eyes again it wasn't Donahue's face she saw, but one that was far less intimidating. The man who was grinning appealingly down at her was much younger and as all-American as apple pie. He was dressed casually in jeans, a wildly flowered Hawaiian shirt, and tennis shoes.

"Hi, I'm John Galbraith, Miss Landon. I hope to hell you're feeling better. Clancy has been spitting like a cat for the last hour or so. He's telephoning the lab now to yell at them for not calling the shots more accurately about your reaction to the drug." He made a face. "Better them than me. I nearly got myself mutilated when I brought you in here in that comatose state."

The breezily casual statement issuing out of that boyishly appealing face shocked her into full consciousness. "*You* brought me here?"

"I get all the really quality assignments," he said sarcastically. "Kidnapping an American citizen was a natural for me."

She sat up in bed. Her dizziness was gone now, though there was still the trace of a headache. "A criminal assignment," she said. "You're going to go to prison for a long time, Mr. Galbraith."

"I won't, you know," he said softly. "Clancy wouldn't have sent me on the job if he hadn't had me covered. He protects his men."

"He'll have trouble protecting himself this time."

A tiny frown wrinkled his brow. "Look, Miss Landon, I know you're upset, but don't make the mistake of going against Clancy. He has no intention of hurting you, but he's not about to let you go until Baldwin surfaces. It will be a good deal pleasanter for you if you'll accept that. Clancy is the toughest bastard I've ever run across. You don't want to cross him."

"The hell I don't." Lisa could feel her anger igniting once again as she remembered the sheer arrogance, the outrageous illegality of Donahue's actions. "At the moment, I not only want to cross him—I damn well want to draw and quarter him." Her voice dropped to an ominously low pitch. "After I finish with you."

Galbraith flinched. "I'm easier meat than Clancy, but I don't think I'd like that. You seem to be a little bloodthirsty at present. I think I'd better feed you." He rose to his feet. "You haven't had anything to eat for nearly twenty-four hours. I'll go to the kitchen and see what I can whip up. You'll find all your clothes in the closet and in the drawers of the bureau." He gestured to a door to the right of the bed. "The bathroom's right there. I'll tell Clancy you're feeling much better . . . well, better enough to create a little mayhem." He was strolling toward the door across the room. "I'll be right back with your dinner."

Dinner? Her gaze flew to the French doors across the room. The sky was flushed with the scarlet and pink of sunset. She must have been unconscious almost an entire day. No wonder Clancy Donahue had been concerned, she thought grimly. He'd probably thought he was going to have to face a murder charge as well as the one for kidnapping. He *would* face those charges as soon as she found a way out of here. There was no way he was going to get by with this!

The French doors. Lisa acted without thinking, tossing the covers aside, slipping out of bed, and running toward the doors. They were unlocked! The tiles still held the afternoon heat and were hot beneath her bare feet as she dashed across the courtyard. There was a brass-bracketed mahogany door in the stone wall surrounding the yard, but she ignored it. Donahue had said there would be guards at all the entrances, but they wouldn't expect her to go over that seven-foot wall. The wall was covered with a thick blanket of fragrant honeysuckle that just might give her enough purchase to climb to the top. She scrambled recklessly up the vines, ignoring the fact that her slight weight was tearing them off the wall. Let Donahue get a gardener to repair the damage. She hoped it cost him a bundle.

When she had reached the top of the wall, she paused a moment to catch her breath—and then lost it again. There were two men below, only a scant ten feet from where she crouched! Their backs were turned to her, thank goodness. If she was lucky . . . The wall bordered a stretch of private beach, and the surf was a hushed roar only a few yards from where the guards were standing. She'd be leaping down onto a soft cushion of sand and they might not hear her. Lisa murmured a fervent prayer, jumped to the ground, and set off running without looking around to see if she'd been heard by the guards.

The familiar skyscraper of the hotel casino towered on the horizon. If she could make it there, surely she could appeal to one of the guests for help, even if most of the staff were under Dona-

ALWAYS · 37

hue's control. She felt a sharp pain in the arch of her right foot as a shell cut into it, but she didn't have time to stop and worry about it.

"Lisa, stop, dammit!"

Donahue! Her heart jerked and then started pounding wildly. Her pace increased, her bare feet flying over the sand.

"Blast it, Lisa, stop! I don't want to hurt you."

Oh, Lord, he sounded as if he were right on top of her. She couldn't go any faster. Her lungs were aching now, and there was an agonizing stitch in her side. The hotel seemed closer. If she could just block out the pain and keep runn—

She pitched forward into the sand, felled by a neat tackle behind her knees. The little breath she had remaining was knocked out of her, and for a moment she struggled wildly to regain it. She was vaguely aware of being flipped over and of powerful thighs straddling her own. Instinctively she started struggling and was immediately punished by having her wrists pinned above her head.

"Give it up!" Donahue's voice was rough. "Don't you know when you're beaten? I realized the second John told me you were awake that I'd better get back to you. I came just in time to see you perched on the wall like a sea gull."

"I'm *not* beaten." She'd gained enough breath back to gasp that out, at least. She tried to lift her leg to knee him, but his weight was too great to budge. "I'm never going to let you beat me, Donahue."

"And to think I was worrying about how fragile you were a few hours ago," Clancy muttered.

"You'd think I would have learned by now how deadly the female of the species can be."

"Let me go!" Lisa tugged desperately, but his grip was manacle hard about her wrists. "I'll show you how deadly I can be. I'm going to murder you, Donahue."

"So John informed me."

"Your baby-faced hoodlum friend?" Her eyes blazed into his. "He at least had the intelligence to believe I meant it."

"If he'd had any intelligence, he wouldn't have left you alone. I told him to stay with you until I came back. I was afraid you'd do something stupid like this when you regained consciousness."

"Stupid? You think trying to escape is stupid?"

"I think fighting any lost cause is stupid," he said harshly. "And this is a lost cause, Lisa. I'm not letting you go."

She had a vague memory of hearing him say something similar before . . . but it had sounded different somehow. Impatiently she dismissed the thought. It had probably been her imagination or that damn drug Donahue had given her. "I'll get away. If not now, then later. I won't let you do this to me."

"Lisa . . ." His blue eyes gazed into her own, and she inhaled sharply as a wave of heat washed over her, drowning her anger with an entirely new emotion. She was suddenly conscious of the power of his muscled thighs as they effortlessly held her own limbs still. He was so big, so powerful; she was so weak and ineffectual by comparison. Her heart started to beat wildly again as if with fear, but it wasn't fear she was experiencing.

No! She wouldn't feel like this. She had heard hostages sometimes developed kinky sexual desires for their captors, but she wasn't like that. Yet her breasts beneath the satin pajama top were moving up and down with the force of her breathing, and she saw Donahue's eyes move compulsively to that betraying disturbance. "Don't fight me," he said hoarsely. She could see his own pulse drumming wildly in the hollow of his throat. "I'd never hurt you. Don't you know that?"

"I don't know anything about you." Lisa closed her eyes to escape the sight of him. That was worse somehow, for now that she couldn't see him, she was more aware of the scents of musk and soap that emanated from him and the burning touch of his thigh through the layers of material that separated them. She opened her eyes again and met his with a fresh sense of shock. So intense. Smoky, intimate, wanting. "I don't want to know anything about you," she murmured.

"I think you're lying." His thumb on her left wrist was absently stroking the sensitive pulse point.

Lisa felt a flash of heat tingle through her. Oh, dear heaven, she doubted if he was even aware of what he was doing to her. A surge of intense desire set her trembling.

"I think you're feeling the same thing I am. In the physical sense, at least, I think you want to know everything about me."

"No, I—" She broke off. It was no use denying it. They weren't children who had no knowledge of sex. She was sure the signs were unmistakable to a man of his experience. "It doesn't mean anything," she said fiercely. "It's a biological reaction that's totally irrelevant. Get off me, Donahue."

"Soon." His gaze traveled lingeringly over the gentle swell of her breasts. Lisa felt an immediate peaking and knew it was visible through the thin satin. She looked at his face, expecting to see triumph. Instead there was only desire and heat and a curious sense of wonder. "How lovely that is. I wish I could see just how beautiful you are."

She felt the air leave her lungs as abruptly as the moment he'd tackled her. "No!"

Reluctantly Clancy pulled his gaze up to meet her own. "No," he agreed. "I know I can't do that. I just said that I wanted to. There's a difference between wanting and taking." He released her wrists. "It's been a long time since I found it necessary to take. I don't think I'd find it satisfying any longer. You don't have to worry about me forcing you into my bed. I want you to want me." His lips tightened. "For God's sake, don't be afraid of me. I couldn't stand that."

She shook her head. "This is insane. Why shouldn't I be afraid of you? You kidnapped me and now you tell me you want me to go to bed with you."

Clancy stood up and reached down to pull her to her feet. "What is there to be afraid of?" He smiled faintly. "You want me, too. I'll wait until you're ready for me. I can be very patient when I want something." He took her elbow and pushed her gently in the direction of the villa. "Don't you think we'd better go back to the house? We have some talking to do."

Automatically she fell into step with him. Why

wasn't she fighting him? His grip on her arm was almost gentle despite its firmness, yet she had the impression any resistance would be instantly quelled. She would have to bide her time until she had another opportunity to escape. She had almost made it. Surely she would succeed in eluding him next time.

"You're suddenly very docile. Are you sure you're all right?"

"I'm not docile." Lisa looked straight ahead. "Like you, I can be very patient when I want something."

He chuckled. "I should have known. My first impression of you was of gentle fragility. Who would have guessed there was such a tigress beneath that serene exterior?"

She felt a little shiver of shock run through her when she realized he was right. She had always been tranquil even in her moments of greatest happiness. Yet she had been acting with a primitive passion that was almost explosive since Donahue had walked into her dressing room. She had never before known fear, rage, or desire in such violent proportions. It made her a little uneasy to realize a stranger could arouse those emotions within her—particularly a stranger as lawless and ruthlessly determined as Donahue.

"What's wrong?" His eyes were narrowed on her face. "Is it something I said? Have I hurt you?"

"No." She avoided his gaze. "What could you possibly have said that would have had an effect on me? Your opinions don't mean a thing to me, Donahue."

His fingers tightened on her elbow. "You have

the tongue of a wasp," he said curtly. "Do you suppose you could keep your stinger out of me until we have that talk? I'm not feeling any too stable myself at the moment."

They had arrived back at the villa and found Galbraith and the other two young men waiting apprehensively at the courtyard door. Galbraith was staring at her with an almost comical look of mournful reproach. "That wasn't very nice, Miss Landon," he said as he opened the door and stepped aside for her to precede him. "You were supposed to be a weak, languishing female, not Sheena of the Jungle, climbing vines and leaping seven-foot walls at a single bound. Now I'm in big trouble."

"You're damn right you are," Clancy said. "You weren't only stupid, you were careless. I'm tempted to send you back to Sedikhan. A rookie operative would have shown more savvy." He jerked his thumb at the two guards. "Replace them, and see if you can find anyone on the island with eyes in their heads." He was propelling Lisa across the courtyard toward the French doors that led to the bedroom. "And until you can find someone, I expect you to roost outside these doors yourself. Understand?"

Galbraith nodded. "I won't be able to replace them until tomorrow. I hope to hell we don't get one of those charming tropical showers tonight."

"Maybe it would wash some sense into that head of yours. Looking like a schoolboy is a professional advantage, acting like one is professional suicide." He ignored Galbraith's grimace as he closed the French doors behind them.

He released Lisa's arm and turned away. "Galbraith won't make that mistake again. You won't even be allowed into the courtyard without permission." He strode toward the door across the room. "This is the only other exit, and I'll be on the other side. I assure you that I'll be a hell of a lot more careful than Galbraith." He looked over his shoulder, and for an instant there was the hint of a smile lighting the grimness of his expression. "I know you better."

"You don't know me at all."

"You're wrong. I don't know you as well as I'm going to, but I do know you." He opened the door. "I'm going to get you something to eat. You'll probably feel better if you wash some of that sand off. However, if you don't feel up to it, I'll be glad to help. It's a valet service I'm always willing to provide when I kidnap a lady." The door closed behind him with a soft, decisive click.

Three

Lisa stared blankly at the closed door. The abrupt
change from brisk, threatening incisiveness to
half-humorous sensuality had once more caught
her off guard. How many sides were there to the
man's personality, anyway? She drew a deep
breath and turned toward the bathroom. Even if
she hadn't felt abominably gritty, she would have
obeyed Donahue's last suggestion. He was too
unknown a quantity for her to be certain that he'd
been joking, and she definitely didn't want to be
exposed to any more intimacies. She was still too
bewildered and wary about her reaction to
Donahue just now on the beach to take a chance of
repeating the scene.

Forty minutes later she had finished showering,
shampooing and drying her hair. Another ten
minutes and she was dressed in baggy white linen

slacks and a loose thigh-length cotton sweater in a warm melon shade. She coiled her hair in a careless knot on top of her head and nodded with satisfaction at her reflection in the mirror. No one could say there was anything in the least provocative about her appearance, and that was just what she intended. She thrust her feet into white canvas sandals and was ready for the fray. For a moment she stood there, trying to gather her composure. She had to come to an understanding with Donahue, and she hoped that understanding would bring them to terms on her release. If she could maintain the same aggressiveness and cool control she had noticed in him, perhaps he would see that she wouldn't permit him to keep her here. The only problem was that aggressiveness wasn't exactly her area of expertise. If it had been, she wouldn't be having this painful dilemma with Martin. She had always been too soft, and Martin had known exactly how to manipulate that weakness to his own advantage.

But Donahue didn't know about that regrettable softness, and if she put up a bold-enough front, perhaps he wouldn't discover it.

Well, she couldn't sit meekly in her own room and wait for Donahue to come to her. That would automatically place him in a position of psychological power. She strode swiftly to the door through which he'd disappeared and tried it. It was unlocked. She threw it open and went in search of Donahue.

The living area of the villa was as quietly luxurious as the bedroom, with thick carpets in a shade of antique gold and contemporary furniture in hues of brown, ranging from deepest chocolate to creamy beige. Everything was sleek, beautifully decorated, extremely expensive, and somehow . . . impersonal. Yes, that was the word. It had the impersonal air of a hotel room.

The kitchen where she found Donahue was equally efficient and impersonal. Stainless-steel and cool blues predominated, but they were no more icy than the glance Donahue threw her as he whirled to face her when she walked through the louvered door. For an instant his face was wary, his stance as ready for action as a cocked pistol. Then he recognized her and obviously forced himself to relax. What kind of experiences and how many years living on the edge of danger had bred that wariness? she wondered with a fleeting sympathy. "I didn't mean to startle you. I just thought we should get that discussion out of the way."

"I didn't expect you." He pointed to the breakfast bar across the room. "Sit down. I've made you a chef's salad and a bacon, lettuce, and tomato sandwich. Do you want coffee or milk?"

"Coffee." She hesitated a moment, then walked over to the navy-blue cushioned stool he'd indicated. So much for her aggressive, businesslike behavior. Donahue was treating her with the casual intimacy of an invited guest, making it impossible for her to respond with the belligerence she would have chosen to display. "This isn't necessary. If you'd just let me go back to the hotel, you wouldn't have to bother with KP duty."

"It's no bother." He crossed the room and set the wooden salad bowl in front of her. "All we have on hand is a bottle of Italian dressing. Will that be all right?"

"Yes, but . . ."

He wasn't listening. He was at the refrigerator taking out a bottle of dressing and a container of cream. He set the two items before her. "I usually make coffee a little strong. I hope that's all right."

"Fine." With barely contained impatience, she watched him pour two cups from the pot on the counter. "I'm not really hungry. I want to talk—"

"Eat. We'll talk later." He smiled faintly. "You'll need your strength."

Lisa cast him a rebellious glance and reached for the coffee. She almost choked as she took a sip. "A little strong! Good Lord, what did you use to brew it? Tar?"

He frowned and tasted his own coffee, then immediately made a face. "Sorry. I've had to have it this strong to keep me awake for the last twenty-four hours. I must have automatically made it the same strength this time."

"You haven't slept for over twenty-four hours?" she asked, startled.

"Closer to forty-eight, not counting the catnap I took on the plane from L.A." He took her cup to the sink and poured it down the drain, then did the same with the coffee in the coffee maker on the countertop. "I'll make a fresh pot."

"Why?"

He glanced over his shoulder. "What?"

"Why did you stay awake? You couldn't have been afraid I'd escape. I was practically a zombie."

"I made you a promise," he said simply. "You seemed worried about . . ." He paused. "About being alone when John brought you to the villa. I promised I wouldn't leave you."

She felt a sudden flutter of warmth, which she was quick to suppress. "That sounds remarkably sentimental for a man in your profession." She looked down at the plate in front of her. "Are you sure you weren't just afraid I'd kick the bucket and leave you to face a murder charge?"

He frowned. "I'm sure. I don't lie, Lisa. If I make a statement, then you can be damn sure it's the truth as I see it. I don't deny I was worried about you, even though the doctor at the lab assured me you'd safely sleep off the effects of the overdose. You could have been more obliging and reacted as they predicted. First you woke up earlier than they said you would. Then you zonked out again and proceeded to sleep like Rip Van Winkle. I've never been so scared in my life as when you decided to oversleep the lab boys' estimate, but it was for you I was frightened, not myself." He reset the strength level on the coffee maker and turned to face her. "Alex told me the other night that he thought I'd finally run across something I couldn't handle. I denied it. I wouldn't deny it today."

She averted her eyes and took a bite of her sandwich. "Not many men could handle a kidnapping with aplomb."

"The kidnapping I can handle. It's what happened between us on the beach that I'm having problems with. I think you know that."

Lisa looked up swiftly and felt a wild tremor run through her. His eyes held the same smoky intensity they had such a short time ago. She felt a slow languid melting sensation in the pit of her stomach. She knew she should look away, but it seemed impossible when the world had narrowed to contain only the two of them. She continued to gaze helplessly across the room at him.

It was Donahue who finally looked away. "You're not eating," he growled as he turned to pour her a fresh cup of coffee. "No more talk until you're finished."

They hadn't really been talking in the last moment or two, but the bands of communication had been loud and crystal clear. Too clear. Lisa immediately grasped the excuse to avoid a confrontation with the exact nature of that communication. "Okay." She took a bite of her sandwich. "Later."

Her throat was so tight she found it difficult to swallow. She managed to finish the sandwich and a little of the salad. She didn't taste much, however, with Donohue leaning lazily against the cabinet and watching her with narrowed eyes. She pushed away the plates. "I don't want any more."

"Good." He straightened. "We can take your coffee into the study. Come on." He crossed the room and lifted her from the stool. She felt a tiny shock of sensation as his hands grasped her waist. She inhaled sharply and hoped desperately he hadn't noticed. She glanced up at him.

He nodded gravely. "I felt it, too. Pretty explosive, isn't it?" He released her and picked up her cup and saucer. "I think we'd better avoid physical contact for the time being. The study is down the hall and to your left."

"All right." Lisa avoided his eyes as she hurried ahead of him down the hall. She was losing confidence by the moment. When she reached the study she chose a wing chair beside the huge mahogany desk and tried to look as businesslike as the room itself. That impersonality was immediately nullified when Donahue handed her coffee to her, then dropped down on the carpet at her feet, leaning against the desk, and linked his hands loosely about his knees.

He stared at her. "I want to go to bed with you," he said softly.

She almost dropped the coffee cup. "That wasn't what I wanted to talk about, Donahue."

"It's the only thing I'm interested in discussing, but we'll touch on the item that's your primary interest first. I can't let you go until Baldwin shows up." He smiled with beguiling warmth. "Discussion closed. Now let's talk about going to bed."

She drew a deep, exasperated breath. "Donahue, I won't deny there's a certain chemical attraction betw—"

"Clancy," he corrected. His eyes were fixed on her face. "I want to hear you say my name." His voice dropped to a velvet whisper. "Say it, Lisa."

She would *not* be caught up in that breathtaking intimacy again. Yet she found herself repeating, "Clancy."

She was rewarded by that same rare smile. "I like that. Thank you, acushla." The faint brogue was more pronounced now and so was the appealing Gaelic charm she'd noticed so fleetingly in the dressing room.

She looked down at the cup in her hands. "I won't let you dismiss the subject so lightly. You behaved outrageously and—"

He suddenly sat upright, kneeling by her chair. "Look, you don't understand." He took the cup from her hands and put it on the floor beside the chair. Then he gathered her hands in his big, warm clasp. "It's not important anymore. Even if I didn't have a reason for using you to lure Baldwin here, we'd have to deal with him anyway. First, because he's making you so damn miserable, and second, because he's a part of your life I have to face and eliminate."

Her eyes widened in shock. "Eliminate? You mean . . ."

He shook his head. "I wish I could, but I know it's not that simple now. There'd always be a cloud hanging over our life if I conveniently 'removed' your first husband."

"First," she repeated dazedly.

He smiled. "First. I'm going to be your next and your last husband. We're going to be married, you know."

"No, I didn't know. This is utterly insane."

"I agree completely."

"We don't even know each other."

"That's definitely a stumbling block, but one that can be easily remedied in this situation."

"You have to be joking." Her eyes were wide in her pale face.

He shook his head. "If I am, the joke's on me. I'm not a boy any longer. I suppose it must seem a little ludicrous to you that a man of my age could fall in love as violently as any teenager, but that's what I've done." He lifted her left palm to his lips and pressed a warm kiss on the soft skin. Holding her gaze with his own, he said softly, "I've fallen in love with you, Lisa Landon. Wildly, passionately, romantically, and with all the accompanying uncomfortable symptoms. I'm jealous as hell, possessive, and miserably uncertain." He shook his head. "You can laugh if you like. I know I must be funny as the devil."

"I don't feel like laughing." Her palm was tingling, burning beneath his lips, and she felt panic racing within her. "You actually mean it, don't you?"

"I told you I didn't lie. Of course I mean it."

She moistened her lips. "I'm not ever going to be married again. Not ever."

"I won't push you. I'll give you the time you need to adjust to the idea," he said quietly. "I just thought I'd better get everything out in the open. This situation is complicated enough without your misunderstanding my intentions." He smiled with surprising sweetness. "My intention is to marry you and love you for the rest of our lives. Is that clear enough?"

Lisa shook her head. "I won't marry you, Clancy. Not if you wait a hundred years." She met his eyes directly. "And I don't love you."

"I didn't expect you to love me. It would have been too much to hope that we'd both succumb to the same insanity." His warm, wet tongue suddenly stroked her palm. "But you do want me. I'm experienced enough to recognize those particular signs. I'll start with that and work my way up."

"No! I won't let you—" She broke off. His teeth were gently nibbling at the smooth tips of her fingers. She felt her heart jerk and then start to pound wildly. "Clancy, stop. I'm not like this. I don't fall into bed with every man who crooks his finger."

"I know that. It was all in your dossier. You haven't been with a man since you divorced Baldwin. After I realized the exact nature of my affliction, I found that very comforting reading."

"That damn dossier." His tongue was licking the hollows at the base of her fingers, and she had to concentrate to bring her thoughts back to the subject. "It's practically indecent to pry into a woman's personal life like that."

"I'll ask Alex to send you mine. It must still be around somewhere. Then we'll be even."

She could see the drumming of the pulse in his temple and felt a sudden urge to reach out and touch that vital life force.

"Okay?"

"What?" He was so warm and alive that she could feel the heat and vitality radiating from his big body, surrounding her, nearly overpowering her.

He grinned. "Why do I feel you aren't paying proper attention to my soulful declaration? Which isn't at all kind, considering that I've never told a woman I was mad about her before."

"You're mad, period. Love at first sight is something out of a storybook. Sexual attraction at first sight I can accept. But love . . ." She shook her head. "It's too farfetched. In a few days you'll be glad I didn't take you seriously."

"Not that farfetched. I've seen it happen before, but I've always been on the outside looking in. I'm familiar enough with the phenomenon to recognize it when it appears on my horizon." He gently touched her lips with his fingertips. "I never thought it would happen to me. I thought I would just go on forever, doing my job and hovering on the edge of relationships, but never really being involved. Do you know what a miracle this is for me?"

She felt her throat tighten painfully. "I'm the wrong woman," she said huskily. "I won't let myself get involved with any man. Find someone else, Clancy."

"I can't. You may be the wrong woman, but you're the only woman."

"I'll hurt you." There was a note of desperation in her voice. "Give it up. I don't want to cause anyone pain, Clancy. There's too much of that in the world already."

"I'll take my chances." His index finger traced the curve of her lower lip. "You have a beautiful mouth. I love to see you smile. It lights up the whole world. You don't do it often enough, though."

"Clancy, for God's sake, *listen* to me."

"I'm listening." His eyes met hers. "Thank you for the warning, acushla, but it's too late. I don't have a choice any longer. I have to try." He smiled faintly. "I must warn you that I can be a fairly tough customer when I go after something, and there will be no holds barred this time. It's a battle I've got to win."

"You can't win, dammit? It's a no-win situation." Her lower lip was throbbing and felt swollen and satin soft beneath the light caress of his finger. That throbbing seemed to be sending out shock waves to every nerve ending in her body. "Let me go."

He shook his head. "I couldn't, even if I wanted to now. We have to finish what we've started."

"We haven't started anything. Now is the time to—" His hands were suddenly at her waist and he pulled her to the floor beside him. "Clancy!"

His blue eyes were dancing. "I have to show you that it's already begun, don't I?" His big hands gently framed her face. "Don't worry. I'm not going to attack. I just want to make a point." His head lowered slowly until his warm breath feathered her lips. He was barely touching her and she could feel the tremors begin to sear through her. He chuckled. "That's not the only thing I want to make, of course, but it will do for a start." His lips touched hers with the greatest delicacy, tasting, brushing, moving, giving her only enough to tantalize without satisfying. His broad chest brushed against her breasts as he shifted position to angle her lips to meet his. She inhaled sharply and felt him hesitate for the fraction of an instant before his lips closed on hers once more. He lifted his head. "Your breasts are exquisitely sensitive, aren't they?" he murmured. "I thought they were." He rubbed his upper body against her with a slow, sinuous movement. She couldn't breathe, and the tremors had centered to become a pulsating ache between her thighs. Her breasts were firming, swelling, and she could feel the hard crest of her nipples thrust against the knit of her sweater. Her eyes closed as she reached for his shoulders to keep herself from swaying. "Earlier, on the beach, I wanted to do this," he said thickly. "And so much more. I wanted to take that satin top off you and just look at you. I wanted to take your nipples in my fingers and make them come alive for me." His hands dropped away from her face to the hollow of her back, arching her up against him. The sound she made deep in her throat was a half moan. "I wanted to use my tongue, my lips, and my teeth." Lisa could hear the heavy pounding of his heart against her breasts, and it triggered a melting somewhere deep within her. She swayed and knew if his hands hadn't been supporting her, her knees would have given way. "I wanted to touch you with every part of me. I still do."

"Please. This is crazy." For heaven's sake, it was the lightest of foreplay and she was about to go up in smoke. She had never before experienced anything even remotely resembling this emotional tempest. "Clancy, this has got to stop."

"I know." His chest labored with the harshness of his breathing as he tightened his arms around her. "It's getting out of hand. Give me a minute."

That was easy to say. The muscles of his chest were still pressed against her, and she could sense his sexual arousal as a living force, swirling in waves around her. There was no aphrodisiac stronger than the knowledge of that arousal. Her hands pressed against his chest. It was a mistake, for now she could feel the heated thunder of his heart against her palms. "Now," she said desperately, opening her eyes to gaze up at him. "Right now!"

He drew a shuddering breath, then his arms dropped away from her and he sat back on his heels. "Okay." The skin was pulled taut over his cheekbones. There was a heavy sensuality curving his lips, and his nostrils were flaring slightly. He looked hungry. . . . Oh, did she look like that, too? He smiled with an obvious effort. "I think the point's been made, anyway. We want each other." His breath released in an explosive rush. "How we want each other!"

"Yes." She raised a trembling hand to brush back a lock of hair from her eyes. "But it doesn't change anything. I'm not about to mistake lust for love. And I'm not about to tumble happily into your bed just because I have a yen for you. I have an idea you'd use that to your advantage."

"Smart lady. I'd do just that." His eyes were twinkling. "But I'd make sure that our advantages were so closely entwined that you wouldn't realize who was using whom."

A wave of heat suddenly rushed over her as she had a sudden mental image of that "entwining." She jumped to her feet. "I think I'd better go to my room. It's time we resumed our roles of prisoner and jailer."

For a fleeting moment she thought she saw a shadow of pain in Clancy's face. It was gone the next instant. She must have been mistaken; Donahue was far too iron tough to allow himself that emotion. "All right. If it makes you feel safer."

There was a hint of desperation in her laugh. "There's something a little macabre about feeling safer as a helpless prisoner."

"You're not the helpless one," Clancy said quietly. "I am. I've never been so damn vulnerable in my entire life."

Her smile faded. He was doing it to her again. Pain, sadness, a yearning to comfort, and the sexual riptide that embroiled them in a whirlpool. "I don't want you to feel helpless," she said with a fierceness that shocked even herself. "I don't want you to feel anything at all for me."

He stood looking at her without answering.

Her hands clenched into fists at her sides. "I won't let you make me feel guilty about something over which I have no control. You're not going to complicate my life. I like it fine just the way it is."

"Do you? Somehow I received the impression that you could use a little help in straightening out one or two aspects." He shrugged. "At any rate, you're going to get it whether you like it or not."

"Clancy, I won't have you marching in and taking me over. Your men might be intimidated enough to put up with that bull, but I won't."

"We'll see. Now you'd better go to your room and rest. I've put you through something of an emotional marathon, haven't I? Just go to bed and sleep on it. Here's the way I think we should handle it. First courtship, then sex, and finally marriage." He grinned. "If you want to rearrange that order, I'm open for suggestions. I definitely can be had."

The inarticulate sound she made was charged with both frustration and exasperation. She turned on her heel and strode toward the door.

"Lisa."

She stopped as she reached for the doorknob.

"We both know we're going to end up in bed together. In another couple of minutes we'd have been making love on that carpet."

Her hand tightened on the knob.

"I just wanted to tell you that I'll try to let you get accustomed to me before we—" He broke off and then continued with rough awkwardness, "Oh, hell, I mean I'll try to be your friend before I become your lover."

She opened the door. "You're not going to be either one. You're just my jailer, Clancy." The door closed firmly behind her.

Clancy uttered a brief but explicit curse. Lord, he certainly had a way with words. It was a wonder she hadn't reacted more strongly to his clumsiness. He had wanted to tell her that he'd be gentle, charming, and considerate. The way it had come out, it had sounded as if he were doing her a favor by not throwing her in bed and jumping her bones. He had thought he'd learned a little diplomacy working for Alex, but evidently it had vanished completely the moment he'd first seen Lisa. All his confidence had disappeared, and he'd felt like a big clumsy oaf of an Irishman with his first woman.

He strode to the cellarette and poured himself a stiff drink. It would probably knock him on his backside as tired as he was, but that might not be a bad thing. At least he would forget what a colossal ass he had made of himself. He drank the brandy down in three swallows and started to reach for the bottle again, then stopped. No, he didn't want to get plastered tonight. Tomorrow he would try to repair the damage his clumsiness had wrought, and he didn't need a hangover to cloud his senses.

Courtship. It was an old-fashioned concept, but one that was very appealing to him. A woman like Lisa deserved not only courtship, but the most careful gentleness and cherishing. Despite her strength and spirit, she gave the impression of being infinitely fragile and fine drawn. When she wasn't smiling there was a somberness about her that filled him with a fierce protectiveness. Pain. There was so much pain behind that tranquil façade. Sometimes he could almost *feel* it beneath the rigid control she exerted. God, he wanted to share that pain. He wanted to share everything she felt, everything she was.

He turned away from the cellarette and moved toward the door. It was going to be an uphill battle all the way to gain her trust as well as her love. He had better try to get some sleep in order to be ready to begin that struggle. Perhaps he'd take her out on the yacht tomorrow. It would get them away from the intimacy of the villa and might put her at ease. He could try it, anyway. At this point, he'd try damn near anything that had even a chance of success.

Four

The sun was marvelously warm on her face, the breeze a soft caress scented delicately with salt and the musk-mint scent she had come to associate with Clancy. Something light fell across her knees, and Lisa reluctantly opened her eyes to see the blue cotton shirt Clancy had been wearing now draped across her outstretched legs.

"Keep covered," he said tersely. "You're too fair to be exposed to a strong sun for long periods without protection. You should have worn slacks instead of those shorts. Don't you ever go to the beach?"

"When I get the chance. New York in the winter doesn't offer many opportunities for sunbathing." He certainly didn't need to worry about burning, she thought as her eyes traveled idly over him. His massive shoulders and broad, corded chest were as deeply bronzed as his face and rippled with power in the afternoon sunlight. The triangle of dark hair, lightly peppered with gray, matted his chest, then narrowed to a thin line before disappearing into the low-slung waistband of his jeans. Lisa felt a sudden tingling in her palms as she wondered what it would feel like to put her hands on that springy cloud. Hurriedly she shut her eyes, closing him out. "Is it very hot in Sedikhan?"

"Yes, it's mostly desert country. The hills can be very pleasant in the summer, though." She could sense that his gaze was riveted on her, and she shifted uneasily in the canvas chair. There was a short silence, and then Clancy said, "Thank you for coming today. I was afraid you'd barricade yourself in your room after I made such a pompous ass of myself yesterday."

"Who would refuse a jaunt around the island on a yacht like this?" she asked lightly. "Particularly anyone as sun-deprived as I am. Besides, being a poor benighted prisoner, I didn't have much choice. You could have just thrown me over your shoulder and carried me on board willy-nilly."

"I wouldn't have done that."

Was there a thread of hurt in his voice? It seemed impossible that she had the power to hurt a man as granite hard as Donahue. Yet he was one of the most boldly honest men she had ever met and so secure in his own manhood that he was unafraid to reveal vulnerability. She had found that out yesterday, to her intense disturbance.

Today he had been very careful to guard against making her uneasy in any way. He had been friendly, charming, and almost impersonal. The hours they'd spent on the yacht had been as golden as the sun pouring down on her right now. She had a sudden impulse to soothe the hurt she had so carelessly inflicted. "I was joking. I know you wouldn't have forced me."

"Good." There was another long, peaceful silence. "May I ask you a question?"

She stiffened warily. "Perhaps."

"Why did you marry him?"

"I'm sure you've seen pictures of Martin. He's a very handsome man . . . quite beautiful, in fact."

"*Why,* dammit? You're not a woman who looks only on the surface."

"I was at that time in my life. I'm afraid I was regrettably naive for a woman of twenty-six. I was an only child and my parents had sheltered me far too much from the realities of life. I grew up thinking I could drift along in that same serene way for the rest of my days, and that everything would be handed to me on the traditional silver platter. Even my singing career was more of a pastime than a vocation."

"Baldwin," Clancy prodded.

"I told you I had the princess mentality. I was twenty-six years old and Prince Charming hadn't bothered to gallop into my life. So I started looking for him." Her lips curved in a bittersweet smile. "Martin appeared to fit the bill admirably. Nordic good looks, charisma, well educated, and he wanted to keep the princess in her ivory tower. It was obviously a marriage made in heaven."

"You didn't know about his illegal activities?"

"A princess can't be bothered to look out the window of her tower except on very special occasions. Didn't you know that? I thought he was in the import-export business."

"He was, in a manner of speaking," Clancy said dryly.

"I didn't find out Martin was a criminal until just after we separated. I had been trying to hold our marriage together for the previous two years, but had finally given it up as a lost cause. My parents had been killed in a plane crash, and I suddenly discovered that there were such things as pain and responsibility in the world. Even a princess has to grow up sometime. I wanted to become a person as well as a wife and mother. Martin didn't understand that and tried to bolt the doors of the tower firmly in place. He refused to accept the fact that I'd finally outgrown my cloistered life-style. He still does, for that matter. He's talked himself into believing that if I come back to him, everything will be the way it was." Her voice lowered to a mere whisper. "Nothing can be the same again. Not ever. Not without—" She broke off and drew a deep, shaky breath. Her eyes opened, but she kept them fixed firmly on the horizon so that he couldn't see their glittering brightness. "You can see why I object to you imprisoning me, Clancy. I've just managed to break out of one jail."

"I wouldn't be like Baldwin. I might want to keep you as my own personal harem girl, but I'm intelligent enough not to try to do it." He paused, then added wistfully, "I hope."

She hadn't mentioned the child. Clancy studied her face, noting the fine-drawn tension of her lips and the air of bleak desolation that surrounded her. He wanted to take her in his arms and hold her, comfort her, but her control was so fragile he was afraid it would shatter. And he couldn't risk that: if she exposed her vulnerability now, she might resent him for it later. His hands clenched on the arms of the deck chair, and he forced them to relax one finger at a time. "I think it's time I told the captain to turn around and go back to the dock. The tip of your nose is definitely pink. You'd better come with me to the bridge. You need to get under cover as soon as possible."

She sighed regretfully as she picked up the shirt draped protectively over her legs and handed it to him. "You're probably right, but I hate to move. Oh, how I love to bask."

"And I love to watch you bask," he drawled. "It could become my favorite outdoor sport. As for indoor sports . . ." He suddenly frowned. "Your legs are pink, too. The shirt didn't do much to protect you."

"The damage was probably done by the time you so gallantly threw it over me."

His eyes were still fixed moodily on her legs. "You don't take care of yourself. You're too thin."

"Chicken legs," she agreed lightly.

"No."

There was a note of thickness in the negative that caused her gaze to fly to his face. His eyes were now hotly intent and his lips held a hint of sensuality. Her heart leapt to her throat and she felt a flash of heat run through her that had nothing to do with the sun.

"No, they're lovely." One big hand reached out and slowly touched her upper leg. She felt a jolt of electricity that made her a little dizzy. "Beautifully symmetrical and well muscled." His index finger moved caressingly to her inner thigh. "Silky. Good Lord, you're so soft and silky."

She should move away from him. She should brush his hand aside with a light remark. Why couldn't she move? Why did she just sit here with that hot, languid heat unfolding within her and the tension building in the center of her womanhood? She felt as if she were mesmerized as she watched his slowly moving finger trace lazy patterns on her flesh.

"Part your legs a little, acushla."

She obeyed without thinking. She didn't seem to be able to think, only to feel. His hands were so big and strong, darkly tanned against her fairness. There was nothing graceful or artistic about the finger that was sending shafts of sensation through her. His hand was as blunt and strong as the rest of the man. The hand of a doer, not a dreamer.

"I like this," he said as he stroked the ultra-sensitive skin with gossamer gentleness. She gasped as his finger slid beneath the edge of her shorts to the apex of her thighs. His finger halted as he heard the tiny sound, and his eyes lifted to meet hers. "I'm rushing you, aren't I?"

He drew a deep, shuddering breath and withdrew his hand, the tips of his fingers lingering reluctantly before he forced them to leave her flesh. "Sorry. I meant to be a perfect gentleman today. I should have known I wouldn't be able to pull it off. I want you too much." There was a flicker of frustration in his eyes as he glanced at her legs, still spread in voluptuous abandon. "But you don't have to be so damn willing, either. How do you expect me to keep my hands off you when you do whatever I ask?"

Her eyes widened in shock and she closed her legs hurriedly.

"Oh, damn, I did it again," he said with supreme self-disgust, and stood up. "For heaven's sake, don't look so stricken. It wasn't your fault. It was mine. I'm one big ache and I'm striking out like the bastard I am. Come on. Let's get you out of the sun." He reached down and pulled her to her feet.

Lisa cast him a bewildered glance as she fell into step beside him. She had been moved from pain to sensuality to guilt in the space of minutes. Now, incredibly, she was feeling sympathy for the man who had inspired all of those emotions. "It was my fault, too," she said huskily. "I guess I was caught off guard. I don't usually behave so—" She broke off. She mustn't tell him that she had never had such an explosive physical response to any other man. She couldn't afford to encourage him in any way. "Let's forget it, shall we? Blame it on this gorgeous tropical sun."

"I don't want to forget it. I fully intend to remember it." He was staring straight ahead, his expression set in lines of grim determination. "Because someday you're not going to have to be caught off guard. Someday you're going to welcome me with joy, Lisa. You're going to be lying naked on the deck in the sunlight and you're going to hold out your arms to me."

She smiled with an effort. "You saw it in your crystal ball, I suppose?"

"No, in my imagination. I'm very good at making

my visions come true. It's all a matter of holding a goal firmly in mind and not giving up."

He shrugged into his shirt but didn't bother to button it. She wished that he had. The sight of those powerful muscles and that cloud of crisp hair was still having a disturbing effect on her pulse rate.

"And I have no intention of giving up," he said, low and firmly.

"Neither do I. So we're at an impasse." She shot him a glance that glinted with a hint of humor. "Besides, I'm not enough of an exhibitionist to enjoy the kind of scenario you've set up for me. This yacht has quite a large crew, doesn't it?"

"Only twelve. But I wasn't thinking of this ship. It's just one of the launches owned by Sedikhan Petroleum. I have a twenty-footer moored at Marasef harbor that can be run by a two-man crew. I thought you'd realize I wouldn't allow any lascivious peepshows. I'm much too possessive to put you on display for the crew's delectation."

She looked away, searching desperately for a safe, impersonal subject. Fat chance. There didn't seem to be such a thing as impersonality between the two of them. "*One* of the launches? Does Sedikhan put many luxury yachts like this at your disposal?"

He nodded. "We keep our own launches and helicopters on most of our permanent possessions. Otherwise, we usually lease what we need. Naturally I have access to anything Sedikhan Petroleum controls."

"Naturally," she echoed. Clancy's statement had been perfectly matter-of-fact. Obviously he had wielded an almost limitless power for so long that it had become commonplace to him. "How long have you been head of security for Sedikhan?"

"Practically all my adult life." He grimaced. "Though I started out as a cross between a tutor and bodyguard for Alex Ben Raschid and his cousin, Lance, when they were teenagers. Old Karim, the reigning head at that time, wanted a man of my particular qualifications."

"Qualifications?"

"I'd batted around the world a bit and been everything from a roughneck on an oil rig in Texas to a mai tai fighter in Malaya. I wasn't much more than a kid myself, but I could handle myself in practically any situation going. In an oil-rich country like Sedikhan, where border skirmishes are a fact of life, that was a blue-chip recommendation."

"I can see how it would be." It was difficult to visualize that wild, tough boy taking on a responsibility that would make a mature man flinch. No wonder he carried his authority so effortlessly. "So Sedikhan is your home now?"

"Yes, as much as any place can be. My job hasn't permitted me to put down any firm roots. Sedikhan is an economically strategic country, and that means there's no way we could remain isolated. In the past I've traveled at least six months of the year." He paused. "That doesn't mean I have to continue to do so. I have some good men in key spots around the world. I can learn to delegate."

She looked out at the water. "You'd probably miss it terribly after all these years. I don't think you should be in a hurry to change your life-style."

"I would miss it, but there are people I love in

Sedikhan. It would be nice to have time to spend with them again."

"Alex?"

"Alex and Sabrina, Lance and Honey, David and Billie, Karim . . ." He smiled faintly. "And so many others. Really wonderful people, Lisa. I want you to meet and know all of them."

There was such warmth and affection radiating from his face that suddenly she wanted that, too. She shook her head sadly. "I'm sure they're as wonderful as you say they are, but I doubt if we will ever meet. Sedikhan is a long way from New York City."

"Not that far. I could order the jet and we'd be there in six hours. Shall I do it?"

She laughed. "Just like that?"

"Yes." He stopped her by placing a hand on her arm. His eyes were warmly intent. "I want to take you home with me. I guess I'm a little old-fashioned. I want you to meet my people. Will you come?"

She shook her head, her expression troubled. "I can't do that. It wouldn't work, Clancy."

"It *will* work." His tone was so rough it startled her. He was silent for a moment, as if trying to get that violence under control. "Look, would it help if I told you I'm a very rich man? Alex has always been very generous with the people he cares about. It's never meant anything to me before, but now I like the idea of being able to give you things. To hell with the ivory tower. I can give you a palace, if that's what you want."

"You'd *buy* me?"

"I'd buy you in any way I could. Money, personal freedom, fame." He smiled a little recklessly. "Do you want to be the next Streisand? I'll get that for you."

She shook her head. "I've outgrown wanting everything served on a silver platter, remember?"

He tightened his hold on her arm. "There must be something in life you want enough to strike a bargain for. I just have to find out what that is, Lisa."

Her eyes widened. "You'd want me that way?"

"No," he said. "I want you as crazily in love with me as I am with you, but I'll take what I can get."

"I think you'd better let me go," she said softly. "I'm very much afraid I'm beginning to like you, Clancy Donahue, but I'll never love you."

He let his breath out in a rush. "Well, that's progress, anyway. At least you don't want to draw and quarter me anymore." He grinned. "Why should I give up now? I never expected it to be easy. Just give me a few days and you'll see that even gruff security men have their charming side."

That was exactly what she was afraid of. She was already finding it difficult to separate her physical and emotional responses where Clancy was concerned. She raised a brow. "You're planning to dazzle me?"

His smile faded. "No, just love you, acushla," he said quietly. "And try to make you love me."

She felt her throat tighten helplessly as she gazed up at him. How could you reply to a man who made statements like that? Particularly when he clearly meant every single word.

His fingers reached up to touch her cheekbone with a featherlike caress. "Never mind. You'll become accustomed to it in time. I am." His hand dropped to her arm and he began to propel her toward the bridge enclosure only a few yards away. "Come on, let's get you back to the villa and out of the sun. We'll have to find something to do indoors for the next day or two. I think you're definitely going to have a sunburn." He grinned down at her with sudden mischief, his white teeth flashing in his dark face. "How are you at checkers?"

Clancy Donahue was a master at the game of checkers.

Lisa soon found out why that smile had been charged with elfin humor. The predicted sunburn had duly appeared by the time she'd showered after they had returned to the villa. Though not particularly painful, it was enough to keep her from wanting to expose herself unnecessarily for a time. In the next two days she found that Donahue was an expert not only at checkers and chess, but at poker and gin rummy as well. He played with a quiet concentration and a boyish zest that made it a pleasure to compete with him even when she lost—something that happened with depressing frequency.

At the end of the second evening of this cruel and unusual punishment, Lisa pushed back her chair and shook her head ruefully. "Skunked again. Where did you learn to play so damned well? I'm not at all sure you haven't lied to me, Clancy. You couldn't have had time to learn all these skills and have a career, too."

"Checkers I learned in a campaign in Southeast Asia when I was eighteen. Karim was a chess fanatic and always looking for someone to play. Philip El Kabbar hooked me on mah-jongg. Poker was always one—"

She held up her hand to stop him. "I'm sorry I asked. Is there any game in which you aren't expert?"

He tilted his head consideringly. "Monopoly, maybe. I've only played that once or twice with Sabrina's son. Do you want me to send to town for a set?"

"Are you kidding? That's a big business game, and you've played it for real in one form or another since you were a kid. We can't play Clue for the same reason." Smiling, she stood up. "I'll think about tic-tac-toe while I make coffee. At least there wouldn't be a winner."

He frowned in sudden concern. "Should I have let you win? I didn't think you'd want that."

She shook her head. "No, I can take it. Though perhaps in a little less massive doses." She turned toward the kitchen. "Next time I get a sunburn I'm going to read and improve my mind."

Clancy rose to his feet and trailed after her into the kitchen. "Next time I may be in a position to keep you amused in other ways. There is a game that has only one rule and everyone wins."

She glanced warily over her shoulder. "What game?"

"Pleasure," he said softly. "Wanna play?"

She looked away. Caught again. Clancy could go on for hours being the perfect companion, teasing, casual, almost avuncular. Then, when she least expected it, he would slip in a remark like that and suddenly she would feel a bolt of sexual awareness that was like a hand stroking her. She wished she hadn't thought of that simile. It reminded her of the times during the last two days when she'd sat across the card table and watched his hands as they shifted a chess piece or drummed lazily on the table as he waited for her to move. Those broad, capable hands that had moved on her thigh, burning her. . . . Quickly she blocked the memory. "You'd probably stack the deck," she said as she crossed the room and opened the coffee cannister.

"Only if it would give you the edge." He sat down on the stool at the breakfast bar. "I don't think you'd mind my letting you win at that game."

Lisa's hand trembled as she measured the coffee into the coffee maker. Suddenly the sexual tension between them was vibrantly alive again. Most of the time she was conscious of it only as a subliminal force, until Clancy chose to strip off the gloves and bring it nakedly to the forefront. Strip. Naked. Damn, she had to keep away from words that brought images to mind. Clancy's broad naked chest feathered with soft springy hair. His hard stomach and powerful thighs.

"You're putting in too much coffee," Clancy said softly. "Unless you've decided you need an overload of caffeine to keep you awake tonight."

"No. I wasn't thinking, I guess." She moistened her lips. She had been thinking too much, blast it. "I don't really want it, anyway. Why don't we just turn in?"

"Okay." He stood up. "You seem a little nervous. Is there something wrong?"

"Jail fever. I need to get out of the house." She turned to face him. "I need to get away from Paradise Cay. Martin hasn't shown up. He's probably half a world away from here. Let me go, Clancy."

He shook his head. "It's just a question of time." He walked slowly toward her. "If you want to get out of the house, I'll take you to the straw market tomorrow afternoon. I hear it's something of a tourist trap, but it will be a change."

"With Galbraith and your other minions trailing along behind?"

"They won't get in the way. You won't even see them if they're doing their job properly."

"But I'll know that they're there." She poured the coffee back into the cannister. "You're sure I can't talk you into putting me on a plane to New York instead?"

He nodded. "I'm very sure. I've never been more sure of anything." He was standing next to her, close enough for her to feel the heat emanating from his body. "Has it been so bad for you the last few days? I thought you were enjoying yourself." His lips lifted in a lopsided smile. "I know I'm not most women's idea of the man with whom they'd like to be stranded on a desert island, but I thought you'd adjusted very well."

Did he really think he wasn't attractive to women? Probably. She had found him remarkably lacking in conceit. "No, it hasn't been bad," she said gently. In retrospect, the last few days had been stimulating, amusing, even challenging. Clancy was keenly intelligent, quick witted, with a marvelous sense of humor and a fine appreciation of the ridiculous. He had a zest for life that blended oddly with the cynicism that his life-style had bred. She'd found herself not only desiring him physi-

cally, but craving his company as well. That reali-
zation was probably what had triggered her sudden burst of desperation. He was coming too close,
and she couldn't risk that. The less intimacy the
better from now on. "You can't blame me for being
a little restless under the circumstances. The
straw market sounds fine."

"Have you been restless?" he asked softly. "So
have I. Do you suppose it springs from the same
cause?" His eyes were narrowed intently on her
face. "If it does, I can suggest a better remedy than
the straw market." His hands reached up to cradle
her face. Warm, capable hands, the pads of his fingers slightly calloused and rough against the
smoothness of her cheeks. Strong hands, yet they
were a little unsteady as they touched her.

She excited him, and the knowledge increased
her own arousal. She was trembling again. It
seemed to be a permanent state when she was
around Clancy. "Not a safe remedy."

"I'd keep you safe. You'll always be safe with me."
His thumbs splayed out, rubbing gently at the corners of her mouth. "As safe as you want to be." His
thumbs moved slowly to meet in the center of her
lower lip. "Sometimes it can be fun to forget about
safety. Haven't you found that?" He exerted the
tiniest pressure and her lips parted. "I can feel the
throbbing of your heart against my thumbs. Your
lips are almost as sensitive as your breasts, aren't
they?"

Lisa swallowed; her breasts lifted and fell with
each shallow breath. The top button of his white
shirt was undone and she could see a shadowy
glimpse of the wiry pelt of hair on his chest. She

couldn't seem to pull her eyes away. She wanted to touch him, comb her fingers through that crisp mat, explore the powerful, heavy muscles of his shoulders. His dark head was lowering slowly. "Take a chance, Lisa," he urged. "Give me your tongue."

He covered her lips with his mouth but exerted no pressure. Waiting. His lips were warm and hard, his breath clean and sweet, but she wanted more. She gave him what he wanted, and she felt him shudder against her. He took her into his mouth, sucking gently, lovingly. She felt his body harden as he pulled her into the hollow of his hips.

Her hands reached out blindly, fumbling with the buttons of his shirt. He went still. Then, without taking his mouth from hers, he brushed her hands aside and unbuttoned the shirt himself. He took her palms and placed them flat against his chest. She made a sound deep in her throat that was half moan, half purr of satisfaction. This was what she had wanted. Her palms tingled as the crispness of him pressed into their softness. She moved her hands slowly, tentatively, savoring the sensation, playing, tangling, tugging.

He was rock hard against her, and the muscles of his chest and belly were knotted with a tension that was almost unbearable. His breath came raggedly in harsh gasps and he was forced to lift his head. He shuddered. "I love your hands on me." His hands tangled in her hair. "But it's not enough. I want your mouth, too, love." He pulled her close so that her cheek was cushioned against the soft hair that had been her playground. The clean smell of soap and man surrounded her, and his skin was warm beneath her lips. Her tongue touched, tasted.

He flinched as if she'd struck him, his fingers twisting in her hair. "Lisa . . ." He moved her lips to another place on his body. "Here, acushla." Then he shifted her again. "And here." He moved her head once more. "Lord, that's wonderful." Suddenly he crushed her mouth to his chest, holding her so tightly that she was breathless. Shudder after shudder ran through him. "Too wonderful. I'm going out of my mind. Let's go to bed!"

She couldn't seem to think. How had they come this far in such a short time? "Clancy . . ."

"I'll make you happy." His hands left her hair and slid down her back in a caressing movement that held yearning tenderness as well as hunger. "Let me try to give you what you need, what we both need. I love you, Lisa."

She felt a little shock run through her as the last words sank home. He did believe that he loved her and this wouldn't be just a pleasant night's romp for him. It would be a step toward the commitment he was trying to wrest from her. The commitment she had no intention of giving any man.

He went still as he felt the unconscious stiffening of her body against him. "Lisa?" He pushed her gently away from him, his hands cupping her shoulders. His gaze searched her face and his expression clouded at what he read there. "No?"

She bit her lower lip. "No," she said. "I'm sorry I didn't stop you right away. I'm not usually a tease, Clancy."

"I know that," he replied. His features were still drawn and hard with hunger. "My fault. I started it. It's been a rough couple of days, and I got a little impatient." He laughed mirthlessly. "But I'm sure I'll be punished for that lack of virtue tonight. I'll probably lie in bed awake and aching all night."

"So will I," she whispered.

"Well, you can just lie there in the same torment that I'm going to go through. I'm not about to give you back those damn sleeping pills."

She shook her head wearily. "I don't want them. I only take them when—" She broke off and turned away. "Good night, Clancy. This situation isn't getting any easier for either one of us, is it? I think you may decide to let me go sooner than you think."

"Don't get your hopes up. I can take a fair amount of punishment. I was once captured by a band of revolutionaries who tortured me every day for three and a half weeks before Alex rescued me. It wasn't nearly as bad as what I'm going through right now, but it did condition me." He inclined his head in a half-mocking bow. "Good night, Lisa. I'll see you at breakfast in the morning."

Five

There was no question about it. It was Martin standing in the half shadow of the awning of the booth across the square.

Lisa felt the blood freeze in her veins, then heat up and start pumping so furiously that she felt a little ill. She cast a swift, surreptitious glance at Clancy standing next to her and breathed a sigh of relief. He was examining a rather flamboyant straw basket with a big-eyed Betty Boop on the side. There was an amused smile on his lips, so he couldn't have noticed either Martin or how upset she was.

Why should he? If she hadn't spotted Martin's idiosyncratic and most arrogant stance, she wouldn't have recognized her ex-husband, either. He was partially hidden behind a stack of rattan chests as well as by the shadow cast beneath the colorful striped awning. But she knew Martin wouldn't allow himself to remain unnoticed: he would approach her with his usual belligerence, and then Clancy would have him. The trap she had been used to bait would snap shut.

"It's pretty campy, isn't it?" Clancy asked, turning to her with a grin. "Garfield the cat, Betty Boop, Mickey Mouse. I told you it was a tourist trap." His amusement faded as he caught sight of her face. "What's wrong? You're pale as a ghost."

She groped wildly for an excuse. "The heat." She smiled shakily. "I feel a little sick. You said I should take care not to overdo. I guess I should have worn a hat."

He frowned with concern. "We'll go back to the villa."

"No," she said quickly. "I'll be fine. It will pass in a minute." She moistened her dry lips with the tip of her tongue. "But I wonder if you could possibly go back to that booth we passed and pick up one of those big straw sailor hats?"

He was still frowning. "I still think—"

"I'll be fine," she repeated. She drew a deep breath and tried to speak calmly. "Just get me the hat, please. I promise not to try to run away. Even if I was tempted to bolt, I'm sure Galbraith has his eagle eye on me."

He nodded. "All right, I'll be right back. Stay out of the sun." He turned away and was soon lost in the crowd.

It had been almost too easy, but she wasn't safe yet. Galbraith would be watching. Her every move should seem natural. She forced herself to pick up the basket Clancy had been looking at and exam-

ine it calmly. She put it down again and then sauntered across the square.

Martin was watching her. She could feel his eyes
on her. She had to concentrate to keep her muscles
from tensing and her steps from quickening with
urgency. Body language. Clancy's men would be
trained observers and she musn't reveal either her
tension or her panic.

She paused by a chest with fancy brass fittings
only a few feet from where Martin was standing.
She shook her head at the eager young boy who
rushed forward to help her. "Just browsing," she
said with a smile. He returned to his chair, picked
up a cardboard fan with the words "Return to Paradise" boldly inscribed in red on its surface, and
began to stir the air lethargically.

She saw a sudden movement out of the corner of
her eye. "No, don't move! I'm being watched."

"I know that." Martin's voice was bitterly sarcas-
tic. "Your new lover must be even more jealous
than I am, Lisa. Bodyguards surrounding the villa,
and you're never permitted to go out without
Desmond's hand on your elbow. He likes to keep
you to himself, doesn't he?" The familiar cold sav-
agery was back in his tone. "You haven't been out
of that house for two days. He must find you very
entertaining."

"You've been watching the villa?" Lisa asked,
startled.

"For three days. I've had a really delightful time
playing voyeur while the two of you were shacked
up in your little love nest by the sea. You seem to
have changed your mind about not having a possessive man in your life. Or does the fact that he

has all that lovely loot make his little foibles all right?"

"Martin, you have to leave. *Now*. You're in danger."

"From Desmond's bodyguards? Did he think that surrounding you with those men would keep me away from you? You belong to me. You'll always belong to me. I have a launch waiting in the harbor. Come with me now, Lisa, and I may decide not to slice up your new lover." He laughed harshly. "You never did understand violence. Well, I understand it and I know how to use it. You wouldn't want him hurt, now would you, darling?"

Clancy hurt? The thought sent a swift surge of panic through her. Then she realized how ridiculous that thought was. Clancy was far more dangerous and intimidating than Martin would ever be. It was Martin who was in danger. "Listen, Martin, things aren't what they appear. I haven't got time to explain now, but you have to get away from Paradise Cay."

"Then come with me." His voice was suddenly low and urgent. "I'm in trouble, but it will blow over soon. You loved me once. Everything will be the way it was, you'll see. I need you, Lisa."

Oh, dear Lord, she couldn't stand this. "The woman who thought she loved you doesn't exist anymore, Martin. I can't give you what I don't have."

"It's the boy, isn't it? You can't forgive me for what happened to Tommy."

"No, it's not Tommy." She tried to keep her voice from shaking. "I know you couldn't help—" She broke off. "Oh, please, Martin. Just *go*."

"Not until you go with me. I can make it up to you. Let me try, baby."

"I'm not a baby. I'm an adult. You never understood that." Oh, merciful heaven, the tears were too close. The memories were too close.

"Desmond must be quite a man. I'm warning you, I'll find a way to get rid of him, Lisa."

"His name isn't Desmond," she said. "That's what I'm trying to tell you. His name is—"

"Isn't this the dramatic moment when I make my entrance?" Clancy asked sardonically. "Just like Hercule Poirot in an Agatha Christie thriller?"

"Clancy!" Lisa whirled to face him.

"I'm afraid you'll have to do without your hat. I thought it was more important that I meet Baldwin."

"You knew?" she whispered.

"It's fortunate you're a singer and not an actress. You'd never make it on the stage." Clancy was looking at Martin with a touch of savage hunger in his eyes. "Aren't you going to introduce us, Lisa? I've been waiting a long time for this moment. I'm Clancy Donahue, Baldwin."

"Donahue!" A flush of rage mantled Martin's classic features. His gray eyes narrowed on Lisa's white face with an ugliness that was nearly tangible. "A setup? You're shacking up with Donahue and trying to hand me to him gift-wrapped?"

"No. I tried to warn you," Lisa said wearily. "You wouldn't listen."

"You didn't try very hard. You wanted to get rid of me and then you and your police snoop of a lover could live happily ever after."

"He's not my lover." She didn't really expect to

convince him. Martin always believed only what he wanted to believe.

"Don't lie to me." Martin's eyes were blazing. "I can see the way he looks at you."

"I am her lover," Clancy said tersely. "You're out of the picture, Baldwin. You're also going to be out of my hair from now on."

"The hell I am." Martin stared at Lisa, smiling coldly. "You shouldn't have done it, Lisa. You betrayed me. Betrayers have to be punished." His voice lowered, grew silky and venomous. "You know, I was glad about what happened to Tommy. I knew you always put him first."

Clancy took a step toward him. "You're not going to punish anyone, Baldwin. If you're extremely lucky, you may get out of this with your skin, but you're not ever to think of hurting Lisa. It would prove fatal."

"Threats?" Martin's lips curled. "You're defending your wh—" His powerful left arm swept forward with a lightning-swift movement and struck the precariously balanced rattan chests. Suddenly the whole stack came tumbling toward them!

Lisa heard Clancy's muttered curse before he pulled her away from the chests that were crashing all around them. She heard the shrill, angry scream of the booth attendant, and then Galbraith was beside them.

"Did you see which way he went?" Clancy asked.

Lisa's gaze flew to the shadowy corner where Martin had stood an instant ago. He was gone!

"Through that alleyway in back of the booth," Galbraith said. "I put Hendricks on his tail."

"Good." Clancy let go of Lisa's arm and turned

away. "I'm going after him. Take Lisa back to the villa." He jumped over one of the chests in his path and took off running.

Lisa gazed after him in a daze. Everything had happened so fast that it was difficult to comprehend.

Galbraith placed a gentle hand on her elbow. "We have to do as Clancy said, Miss Landon. Don't worry. Everything will be fine. Clancy will catch the bastard."

It was what would happen when he did catch Martin that was turning her panic to terror. There had been so much ugliness, so much menace in Martin in those last minutes. How could he have said that about Tommy? She could feel the sheer horror of it turn her cold and sick. She'd been so sure that guilt and desperation had caused Martin's obsessive behavior toward her. Could she have been that mistaken?

"You're shaking." Galbraith frowned in concern. "Are you okay? Clancy will have my severed head in one of these baskets if he comes back and finds you sick."

"I'm all right." She wasn't all right. She could feel the dark, tattered edge of that familiar depression closing in on her, and her footsteps quickened as if to run away from it. But she knew it was useless. She hadn't been able to escape from it for the last three years. How could she expect to do so now? "Let's just get back to the villa."

It was almost dusk when Clancy returned to the villa, but Galbraith had not bothered to turn on the lights. He was lounging in one of the big easy chairs in the living room, his leg swinging lazily over the wide arm.

Clancy flipped on the ceiling light as he strode into the room, and Galbraith straightened up. "Did you get him?"

Clancy shook his head. "Hendricks lost him in the alleyway." He rubbed the back of his neck wearily. "We spent the entire afternoon searching the whole damn island for any sign of him. We finally tracked down a lead to the Coast Guard office. A man of Baldwin's general description sailed a launch into the harbor three days ago and has been berthed at the dock ever since."

Galbraith gave a low whistle. "He's been living on the boat, then. No wonder we didn't get a tip-off from one of the hotels on the island."

"Well, the launch is no longer in its berth, so it's safe to assume Baldwin's gotten away clean as a whistle. It doesn't matter. I'll still get him." He shifted his gaze to the door of the master bedroom. "How is she?"

"Not good," Galbraith said with a frown. "What the hell did the bastard say to her? She seemed to be in a state of shock. Did he threaten her?"

Clancy's lips tightened. "Yes, but I don't think that's what's causing the upset. Did she eat dinner?"

"I ordered something sent over from the dining room of the hotel, but she didn't touch it." Galbraith flexed his shoulders and sighed. "I don't like it, Clancy. She's too damn quiet. I used to see guys in Nam like that." He smiled crookedly. "Those were the ones who usually ended up wandering off into the jungle or developed a liking for Russian roulette."

Clancy felt a chill touch his spine. He, too, had seen men who had repressed pain and horror until it had become a land mine inside them. "I'll try to get her to eat later. I won't need you for the rest of the evening, John. You can tell the other guards they needn't come back tomorrow."

Galbraith's brows rose in surprise. "The surveillance is officially over? I thought you'd continue it for a few days in case Baldwin decided to come back."

"I don't doubt that he'll be back, but he's not stupid enough to make it anytime soon. He knows we're waiting for him. My guess is that he'll wait and try to catch us by surprise."

Galbraith nodded in agreement. "You think he'll still try to make trouble for Miss Landon?"

"I don't think there's any question about it," Clancy said bitterly. "Thanks to the little scenario I set up, he's not only an annoyance but an actual threat to her now. He thinks she's betrayed him, and there's no telling what a psycho like that will do to get revenge."

"Then she'll remain under Sedikhan protection indefinitely." It was a statement, not a question. Galbraith got to his feet. "Do I put her on a flight to New York tomorrow and arrange for an operative to cover her there?"

"No, I don't think so. I'd have to put a battalion around her to keep her safe in a heavily populated area like New York." Clancy frowned. "I may have to take her to Sedikhan."

"The lady may decide she's tired of being pushed

around from pillar to post at your convenience."
Galbrath's lips curved in a faint smile. "She could
have a few ideas of her own. We can't keep her a
prisoner forever."

"I don't want to keep her prisoner at all. Damn,
I'm tired of this mess."

Galbraith shrugged and moved toward the door.
"I'll report back tomorrow and you can let me know
what you've decided. Good night, Clancy."

"Good night." Clancy stood staring absently at
the door for some minutes after it had closed
behind Galbraith. God, he was scared. He knew
what he had to do was necessary, but that didn't
make it any easier. His hands clenched into fists at
his sides. Do it, he told himself. Get it over with,
dammit.

He turned and strode to the master bedroom and
knocked briskly. He didn't wait for an answer but
opened the door and walked into the room.

Lisa was at the French windows gazing out into
the courtyard, silhouetted against the last rays of
twilight.

"He got away," Clancy said. "I'm sure you'll be
glad to know your conscience is entirely clear.
Baldwin is somewhere on the high seas by now."

"I know you're disappointed," Lisa said, not
turning around. "It's not that I condone what he's
done, but I couldn't be responsible for—"

"I know why you did it. I'm not blaming you. I do
think you should develop a better sense of self-
preservation. You heard what he said to you before
he took off. You're on Baldwin's hit list from now
on."

"Yes," she said dully.

He drew a deep breath. It was worse than he'd thought: her voice was totally apathetic. "I've sent the guards away."

She didn't answer.

"For God's sake, say something," he burst out. "What the hell is wrong with you? I feel like I'm talking to a statue."

"I'm sorry. I'm very tired," she said like a polite little girl. "I'd like to go to bed now."

"Not now. We need to talk."

"I'm very tired," she repeated. "I'd like my sleeping pills, please."

"The hell you would!"

"It's all over. You said you'd sent the guards away. The pills are my property and I'd like them returned."

"It's not all over, and if you think I'll let you take—"

She whirled to face him. He couldn't see her face in the dimness of the room, but her body was as tense as an arched bow. "Give them to me. I *need* them, damn you!"

"All the more reason not to give them to you. It's time you stopped hiding behind them, Lisa. It's time you came out into the light and faced it." He kept his voice hard with an effort. He could feel her pain and desperation radiating in waves across the room. "I'll help you in any way I can, but we've got to come to grips with the problem first." He moved to the bedside lamp and turned it on. For a moment he wished he hadn't. So much pain, so much emptiness showed on her pale face. "Lisa, we have to talk about it. You can't go on like this."

Her eyes widened in sudden fear. "You don't

know what you're saying. It's none of your business what I do, anyway. Leave me alone, Clancy."

"I can't do that. Do you think I want to bully you like this?" His eyes met hers. "Tell me about Tommy, Lisa."

"No!" She turned her back on him, staring out the window. "Get out, Clancy."

"Your son, Tommy, was born one year after your marriage to Baldwin. According to your file, you and the boy were extraordinarily close. He died in an automobile accident three years ago. Baldwin was driving and received only a slight concussion." Her spine was painfully rigid, as if he were flogging her and she had to tense to bear the blows. Lord, he was glad he couldn't see her face now. "You came very close to a nervous breakdown. You were under a doctor's care for six months, and then you resumed your career and concentrated all your energies on that area of your life."

"You have all the facts down accurately," she said, her voice brittle. "You don't need me to tell you anything."

"Yes, I do. I need you to tell me about Tommy. What did he look like? Was he blond like Baldwin?"

"No, he had brown hair, acorn brown. What difference does it make?"

"Brown eyes?"

"No, they were hazel." Her voice was a mere whisper. "Please, don't do this to me, Clancy."

"What was his favorite color? Most children like red."

"He loved yellow. Bright yellow. For his fifth birthday I arranged a party at his nursery school, and he wanted all the balloons to be yellow."

"Was he a quiet child?"

"Sometimes. When he was tired, he'd bring his favorite book and curl up next to me in the same chair." She seemed to be struggling to get the words out. "He'd lean his head against me and not say a word until I'd finished. Though most of the time he'd fall asleep before I got halfway through."

"Did he have a favorite toy he slept with?"

"Bruiser. It was a tattered old panda bear with one black eye. I told Tommy he looked like a punch-drunk fighter. It got so worn I tried to get him to accept a replacement, but he loved it so. . . ."

"What happened to Bruiser, Lisa?"

She didn't answer. Her spine was arched with unbearable tension as if she were being stretched on the rack.

"Tell me, Lisa."

"He's with Tommy." Her voice was so faint he could hardly catch it. "I wanted him to have something he loved with him. Bruiser is with Tommy."

Oh, God, he couldn't keep this up. Why wouldn't she break? "What did Tommy look like when he smiled?"

"He had a dimple in his left cheek and he'd just lost his front tooth. I was planning on having his yearly picture taken, and I told him he'd look as ragtag as Bruiser. He laughed and—" She whirled to face him. Tears were running down her cheeks and her eyes were wild with grief. "But I never had that picture taken. He died, Clancy. He *died*!" Her slender body was suddenly racked with sobs. "It wasn't fair. Tommy was so good. He didn't deserve to have that happen to him."

Clancy crossed the room in three strides, and

gathered her in his arms. His hands cradled the back of her head, pressing her face into his chest in an agony of tenderness. "I know, acushla. I know."

"He was a miracle." Her voice was muffled, but the words flowed on. It was as if once started, they were impossible to halt. "A miracle. I hadn't done anything to deserve him. I'd always been a little selfish and thoughtless, yet I was given Tommy. He was so sweet and affectionate. And smart. He was very bright for his age. All his teachers said so." Her hands clenched his shirt front, wrinkling it. "I *loved* him so, Clancy."

He could feel his throat tighten painfully. "The dreams. What are the dreams about, Lisa?"

"Tommy. They're always about Tommy, and they're all the same. It's late at night and I'm at home. I'm happy. I even hum a little as I climb the stairs. I have to tuck Tommy in for the night, and I always love doing that. He's always so clean and sweet after his bath. Then I open the door and Tommy's not in his room. I don't understand and I walk into the room and go across to his bed. The bed is very neat and cold and perfectly made up, with not a wrinkle in the bedspread. And I look down at it and I know that it's going to stay that way. That Tommy's never going to be there again. That I'm never going to tuck him in, or kiss him good night, or hold him. . . ."

He rocked her, pain exploding inside him. God, what must it be like for her? "I think I would have murdered Baldwin myself, if I were you," he said huskily.

"I thought he felt the same way I did. He never

seemed very affectionate toward Tommy, but after we separated he appeared to change. He'd take Tommy out for the day to amusement parks and the zoo. After the accident he seemed so . . ." She paused. "Broken. And he was so concerned when I was ill." She shook her head in bewilderment. "Oh, I don't know."

"He would have realized that his only chance with you was to fake the same bereavement you were feeling," Clancy said grimly. "He didn't sound any too guilt-stricken this afternoon."

"No, he didn't." She couldn't seem to stop the tears from running down her cheeks, but the sobs had begun to subside. "I don't understand it. I don't understand *him*."

"Well, I do," Clancy said. "I understand the bastard very well." Suddenly he picked her up and carried her across the room toward the chair. "But I have no intention of talking about Baldwin now." He sat down on the chair and cradled her on his lap. His hand stroked the fine hair at her temple with gentle fingertips. "That's not what you want to talk about now, either, is it?"

"No." She nestled her cheek closer. "That's not what I want to talk about."

"Tommy?"

"Yes." Incredibly, after all these years, she did want to talk about Tommy. It was as if a festering sore had been lanced and must now be purged.

"Then tell me." His arms tightened lovingly about her. "Tell me all about Tommy. Make me know him, Lisa."

And she did. Once she started, the words refused to stop. She lay there in his arms, her voice almost dreamlike as she rebuilt a world that she'd thought she had lost forever. It was not without pain. The tears flowed and ceased and flowed again as hours passed and pictures of the past flickered, became real, and then faded once again.

Clancy was silent, listening, and only his hand moved as he gently stroked her temple.

Finally the words ceased and Lisa was also silent. She lay curled against him like a weary child, drained, empty, but curiously at peace. She didn't know if it was fifteen minutes or an hour later when she broke that silence by whispering, "Thank you."

His arms tightened around her. "Don't thank me. Tommy is a part of you, and you shared him with me. You were the one giving gifts." He paused. "Is it better now?"

"Yes."

"Good." Another silence. "There isn't any way I can justify what happened to Tommy. I don't intend to, acushla. I can only share something I've learned over the years." His voice was unsteady. "I've lost quite a few people I've cared about. I've led a violent life, and I suppose it was inevitable. It never makes any sense, but it happens. When someone is taken from me, I try to use that grief."

"*Use* it?"

He nodded. "After I've accepted it, I try to channel all the memories and the love and let it flow to someone else. I guess it sounds a little strange, but I feel if I give enough of myself, enough of what I've been given by the one I've lost, somehow some part of that person will still survive. I don't have any real family anymore, but I have my friends in Sedikhan. Every time something happens, I give them more love, more protection, more caring." He grimaced. "By this time, all of them should be pretty well weighed down with it. Sort of weird, huh?"

"No, not weird at all," she whispered. "Beautiful."

"Well, it helps me, anyway. You might try it." He dropped a feather-light kiss on the top of her head. "Now I think I'd better let you get some sleep. You're exhausted." He stood up with her still in his arms and carried her over to the bed. He didn't bother to try to undress her, but settled her on the pillows and pulled the sheet over her.

"You're leaving?" She didn't want him to go. Something had happened in this room tonight. Intimacy had been established; bonds had been forged. In a strange way, she felt that if she had given him Tommy, she had also given a portion of herself. As for what he had given her . . . it could never be measured.

Clancy shook his head. "I'll stay right here." He turned out the lamp, then lay down on the bed beside her and took her in his arms. "I don't think the dreams will come, but I'll be right here to stop them if they do."

She didn't think they would come, either. He had given her so much; she should really send him away. "You don't have to stay. I'll be all right now."

His lips brushed the delicate skin at her temple. "Go to sleep," he said. "I want to stay."

She sighed contentedly and nestled against his hard strength. So hard, so strong, yet with a core of sensitivity and simple beauty that had shaken her profoundly. She was too tired to think of his words right now, but she knew she would soon and that they would bring her comfort. Giving. That's what he had said. Memories that constantly enriched, giving love and beauty to someone else, forming a chain that would last forever. . . .

Lisa's breathing grew deep and even. She lay curved against him with the confiding trust of a little child. Thank heaven she'd fallen asleep so easily. Clancy knew he had taken a big risk tonight. There'd been a possibility that his instincts were wrong, that bringing the tragedy into the open would have done more harm than good. There had also been the chance that even if she'd recognized the necessity of his action, she'd have hated him for the pain he had caused. Neither of those things had happened, thank God.

He stroked her hair, staring absently into the darkness. Lisa was so alone, he reflected. He had tried to comfort her with his own philosophy, but he realized it might not apply in her case. Her dossier had stated that she had no close friends or relatives. Her parents were dead. Very possibly it was her isolation that kept her grief so raw and painful and caused her to turn inward and dwell on her loss. There had to be some way for him to help her conquer that isolation.

Clancy could feel the weariness dragging at him, and he steeled himself against it. He was almost as emotionally exhausted as Lisa, but he couldn't give in to it. Tonight he had stripped away the protective barrier against pain that she had built so carefully. By the time she awoke he had to be ready to give her something to replace it. He settled her slender body more closely against his own with instinctive protectiveness and tried to concentrate his thoughts on what that elusive something would be.

It was still dark when Lisa awoke, and she was immediately conscious that Clancy was no longer beside her. It didn't alarm her. He had promised he would stay with her, and he wouldn't leave her. She didn't even question that instinctive and complete trust. It was just there. She sat up and brushed a tendril of hair away from her face. "Clancy?"

He was standing by the French doors. She could see the glimmer of his white shirt in the darkness. Then she saw the glimmer move and knew that he had turned to face her. "I'm right here. Everything's fine."

She knew that; she was experiencing a sense of peace and serenity she hadn't known for a long time. "Didn't you sleep at all?"

He came toward her. "I wasn't tired. Besides, I had some thinking to do. How do you feel?"

"Good," she said softly. "And very grateful. What time is it?"

"A little after three in the morning. Would you like to go back to sleep, or do you think you could eat something? You haven't had anything since breakfast yesterday."

"You and Galbraith are certainly concerned about my eating habits," she commented. "Perhaps I should furnish you with a few statistics documenting that thin is healthy." She shrugged. "I suppose I could eat something. I'm certainly too wide awake to go back to sleep." She threw aside the sheet. "But first I want to shower. I feel terribly slept in."

"All right." He flipped on the lamp by the bedside table. "I'll make an omelet for you while you shower."

"Fine." She hopped out of bed and crossed to the bureau. Pulling out underthings, slacks, and a loose green tunic blouse, she headed for the bathroom. "I'll be ready in fifteen minutes."

But when she came out of the bathroom fifteen minutes later, Clancy was still in the bedroom. He had flung the French doors wide and stood in the doorway looking out into the courtyard.

"Clancy?" She walked slowly toward him. "Is there something wrong?"

"No." He turned and gave her a reassuring smile. "I just thought we'd talk first. Is that all right with you?"

"Yes, of course." There was something about Clancy's demeanor that made her uneasy. "What is it?"

"I've been doing some thinking tonight." He took her hand and drew her out into the courtyard, where the heavy scent of honeysuckle and hibiscus drifted on the soft tropic air. "I've gone over everything time after time, but I can't come up with any other solution. I want you to know I'm not thinking of myself, though it will give me something I want, too. I honestly believe this is what you need."

"Clancy, I don't know what on earth you're talking about," she said. The lamplight from the bedroom was streaming through the open French doors, and she could see that Clancy's features were set and a bit grim. She laughed a little shakily. "For a man who's usually so blunt, you're certainly beating around the bush, Clancy."

"That's because I'm scared as hell." His hands cupped her shoulders and he pushed her down on the rim of the mosaic fountain. "I don't know how you're going to take this."

"Take what?"

He drew a deep breath. "Do you believe I love you?"

A shock ran through her, and she hesitated. "I believe you think you do," she said slowly.

"Do you trust me?"

She didn't have to think about that. "Yes."

Suddenly he was on his knees beside her, gathering her hands in his. "You should trust me. I'd never do anything to hurt you. Do you remember what I told you about the way I sublimate the pain of loss?"

"Yes," she said, and her hands tightened on his. "I remember."

"But you don't have anyone to turn to and channel that pain, Lisa. You don't have anyone you really love."

"What are you trying to say?"

"That you need *someone*." He glanced up, his expression gravely intent. "I'm saying that I'd like very much to give you a child."

She inhaled sharply. "A child!"

"I'm not suggesting that Tommy could ever be replaced. Every human being is unique and irreplaceable, and what you feel for Tommy is beautiful and special. But you still need someone else to love." He smiled a little crookedly. "I'm selfish enough to wish it could be me, but that's not in the cards. At least not yet. But the need still exists, and I know you'd love your own child." He brought her palm to his lips and kissed it. " Please. Let me give you that child."

"Clancy . . ." Her thoughts were a wild, whirling jumble of fragments.

"I'm not asking any commitment from you. You don't even have to marry me, if you don't want to. The child will be completely yours. I'll sign papers swearing to that." He was silent for a moment before adding haltingly, "I would like you to stay with me until the child is born, if you can see your way clear to do it." His lips twisted in a self-mocking grimace. "You know what a protective bastard I am. I'd worry about both of you, if you weren't right under my nose."

"It's crazy," she declared softly. She felt an odd, glowing warmth deep within her that had something to do with the way Clancy was looking at her with that touching little-boy earnestness. Just as Tommy had looked at her when he'd done something wrong and wasn't sure how she'd react. She stiffened with surprise when she realized how naturally the thought had come. Not with that familiar jolt of pain, but gently, as if Tommy were still with her. Perhaps now that Clancy had freed her from that icy trauma, Tommy would always be with her.

"Not so crazy," Clancy said, playing absently with her fingers. "You want me, so that should make the sex part tolerable."

Lisa almost burst into an hysterical giggle at that. Considering the sexual tension that had existed between them in the last few days, the word "tolerable" was scarcely appropriate.

As Clancy continued to enumerate the advantages one by one, like a solemn-faced child reciting a lesson, she was once more reminded of Tommy. No pain again. It was becoming easier all the time. "I'm rich enough to provide for you comfortably," he continued, "and naturally I'd support you handsomely. You wouldn't want for anything, Lisa, after the baby was born. I realize you will continue your career and would need to arrange for reliable domestic help." Suddenly he frowned. "If you go on tour, I'd like you to send the child to Sedikhan while you're gone. I don't like the idea of the baby being without one of us for long periods of time."

"You've thought all this out very thoroughly," she said quietly.

"It was a long night, and I knew you'd need a solution to the new questions I'd raised. It was my job to give it to you."

So he had given her his solution. Generously, selflessly, with the open-handed simplicity she had come to associate with him. "Clancy, where the hell is *your* sense of self-preservation?" she asked. "What are you getting out of all of this?"

"Quite a bit." He smiled. "At least nine months of you in my bed and in my life. A child that I can love, even though he won't be completely mine. I can live with that. Before you came into my life, I didn't think I'd ever have a child at all."

She felt tears brimming behind her eyes as she remembered the sweetness and wonder she had known with Tommy. Clancy should experience what she had; he would make a wonderful father—

gentle, protective, wise. He shouldn't be cheated out of that joy. "I couldn't do that to you."

He shook his head. "Don't you see? It would be a gift like the one you gave me when you told me about Tommy. There would be no guilt on either side." He kissed her palm again. "Fair exchange, Lisa."

"Not fair at all. I'd be taking. You'd be giving," she said. "I'd have to be even more selfish than I was in my ivory tower days to take you up on a proposition like that."

"You're wrong." His hands tightened on hers. "So wrong. Believe me, there's no way I'd feel like a martyr if you accepted this proposal. I'd feel lucky as hell."

"Then you're an idiot!" Her voice broke and she had to wait a moment before she could speak again. "Clancy, I don't want to talk about this any more right now."

"All right." He gave her hands an affectionate squeeze before releasing them and rising to his feet. "We'll drop it for the moment, but there's one question I'd like to ask first. Would you like to have a child?"

Would she? When Clancy had first said he wanted to give her a child, she had experienced shock and then sheer heady joy. She'd realized after Tommy was born that she was a woman with a strong maternal drive and needed a child to complete her. Motherhood had brought joy and warmth and love. But it also had brought shock and an unbelievable pain. Could she risk that pain again? "I don't know." Her hand moved in a gesture of helplessness. "I'm so confused. There are so many things . . ."

Clancy nodded his head. "I know that. It's a decision that no one can make but you." He turned away. "Think about it. I believe it's the answer for both of us. Let me know when you've made up your mind." He glanced back over his shoulder. "I suppose you don't want that omelet now?"

Food? She shook her head. "You've given me too much to digest as it is."

He smiled. "If I'm going to fatten you up, I'd better schedule discussions like this after you've eaten."

"Oh, I don't know," she said dryly. "A fattening-up would definitely be the result if I yielded to your persuasion on the topic of this particular discussion."

He chuckled. "You're right." His expression grew serious. "I'd love to see you pregnant with my child. There's nothing more beautiful than a woman with that particular bloom on her."

His eyes were so intent that she felt suddenly breathless. "You certainly have weird ideas on female allure. As I remember, the only bloom I noticed when I was carrying Tommy was in my stomach. I looked like I'd swallowed a watermelon."

"I'd like to see you like that," he said softly. "Think about it." He turned and walked into the house.

How could she help but think about it when her head and emotions were whirling like a top? Did she want another child? Was it fair to take from Clancy, even though he said it was what he wanted? *If* she had a child, would she be able to take it and walk away from Clancy? Every instinct rebelled against that last thought. She couldn't hurt anyone like that. Particularly not Clancy, who was kind and honest and loving. She couldn't walk away from Clancy at all.

She stiffened as that last thought emerged haphazardly from the tempest in her mind. Then it solidified into a conviction of unshakable certainty. She didn't want to leave Clancy Donahue, no matter what the circumstances. She wanted to live with him and bear his children and have him smile down on her with that rare warmth until the day she died. Love. She loved Clancy. It shocked her as deeply as his proposition had earlier. Why hadn't she realized she'd been tottering on the brink in the past days? Oh, Lord, now she was more confused than ever.

Lisa stayed in the courtyard for hours, staring into the darkness, lost in thought. It was only after the first streaks of dawn lit the sky that she began to know a sense of peace. The decision had been made. It was a decision that both frightened and elated her. There was nothing like going for broke, she thought as she stood up. Not only was she going to run the emotional risk of another pregnancy, she was about to accept the even greater challenge of being in love for the first time in her life. She was stiff from sitting on the rim of the fountain and so exhausted from strain she felt a little dizzy. She would have loved to collapse on her bed and go to sleep, but she knew she couldn't do that. Clancy deserved an answer from her as soon as possible.

She wanted the child. She wanted Clancy. Those

two facts had become clear in the previous hours. Yet the knowledge of her love for Clancy had come so quickly that she was still uncertain. What if she told Clancy she loved him and found out later she had mistaken sex and gratitude for something deeper? She was a complete novice at this love business. What she had felt for Martin hadn't even come close to what she was feeling now. It wasn't fair to Clancy to make any admissions until she was absolutely sure. And what if Clancy discovered after he made love to her that sex had really been the attraction for him? Then he'd be trapped in a relationship he no longer wanted. Something she knew all about, she thought wearily. No, for both their sakes she'd best move cautiously.

She walked across her bedroom and through the foyer to the guest room Clancy had been occupying since he'd brought her to the villa. She drew a deep breath to steady herself as she paused outside the door. Then, without knocking, she turned the knob and opened the door. The drapes were closed, retaining the darkness of night in the room. She could barely discern the outline of his long body lying beneath the sheet in the large bed across the room.

"Clancy?"

"I'm awake," he said quietly.

She swallowed hard. "I do want to have a child. I want to have *your* child."

He didn't speak for a moment, and she wished she could see his expression. What if he'd changed his mind and had been lying here cursing his idiocy in making that offer?

"I'm glad," he said, his voice thick.

He hadn't changed his mind! She felt a wild surge of joy rush through her. "Only I don't think the terms were fair. I think we should sign a contract stating that we'd each get custody six months of every year."

"Whatever you like."

"And I'll support myself and the child when he's with me."

"I don't think that—" He broke off. "We'll talk about it later. You're very sure?"

"Yes, I'm very sure." Dear heaven, she loved him so much.

"I'll order the jet for later this morning. You'd better go to bed and get some sleep now."

"Jet?"

"I'm taking you to Sedikhan. I'm taking you home, Lisa."

Six

"Coffee?" John Galbraith stood before her holding out a Styrofoam cup, carefully balancing himself against the vibration of the plane.

"Yes, thank you." Lisa accepted the cup, pushing the blanket from around her shoulders to her lap. "I certainly need something to wake me up. I must have been sleeping for hours. Where's Clancy?"

"In the cockpit radioing instructions to Marasef." Galbraith dropped into the seat beside her. "We should be arriving there within the hour."

Then she had been sleeping for almost five hours. It wasn't really surprising. In spite of Clancy's excellent advice, she had been unable to get to sleep immediately. Once she'd gone to bed she had found herself wide awake, her mind zinging and hyperactive. Yet as soon as they'd boarded this luxurious private jet and were airborne, she had fallen asleep as suddenly as if she'd been hit by a sledgehammer. "Do you live in Sedikhan?" she asked Galbraith as she took a sip of her coffee.

"I live where Clancy tells me to live," he said with a shrug. "It's a job that requires a good bit of traveling."

"That's what Clancy said." He had also said he could cut out a good deal of that traveling, she remembered with relief. Perhaps she would be able to travel with him at least some of the time when he did have to go. "Does Clancy have an apartment in Sedikhan, too?"

Galbraith shook his head. "He has quarters at the palace. He usually finds it more convenient to be close to Sheikh Ben Raschid."

Oh, dear, she had never considered where they would live. She wasn't sure she'd like living in a royal palace.

"Go up front with the pilot, John." Clancy was standing beside them. There was an air of leashed tension about him that was nearly palpable. She'd been aware of that edginess during their preparations for departure but hadn't thought it strange. It was a big step for both of them, and she was nervous about this trip, too.

Galbraith got to his feet with a grin. "I have the distinct feeling that I'm not wanted. I always was quick on the uptake." He sauntered down the aisle toward the cockpit.

"Is something wrong?" She set the coffee cup on the table beside her.

"Yes." He sat down in the chair Galbraith had

just vacated. "There's something definitely wrong."

"What?"

"What the devil do you think?" he asked. "Last night you told me you were going to have my child. Now to have a child it's necessary to perform certain anatomical functions. I couldn't think of anything but those functions after you left me this morning. Not that it was different from any other night since I've met you. Then we get on board the plane and you proceed to fall asleep."

She felt the breath catch in her throat. "You wanted to make love to me on the plane?"

"I want to make love to you anywhere I can," he said harshly. "I'm hurting, damn it. I've never wanted a woman like this before." He distractedly ran a hand through his hair. "And now you're going to think that all I said last night was just to get you into bed. It's not true, but I'm . . . What are you doing?" His eyes were on her fingers, which had moved to the front of her blouse and were calmly unfastening the buttons.

"You want to make love," she said as she undid the last button. "We don't have much time, but I'm quite willing. No one will disturb us, will they? You were sharp enough with John to guarantee he won't come back until he's called."

"No one will disturb us," he said thickly. His eyes were fixed on the front of her opened blouse. He could see tempting glimpses of her smooth, pale stomach and the upper swells of her breasts encased in a lacy bra.

"That's good." Her hands were on the front clasp of the bra. Suddenly it was loose and her breasts tumbled free, veiled only by the silk blouse. She smiled at him mischievously. "Well, shall we make a baby, Mr. Donahue?"

His eyes were hot and smoky as they clung to the full mounds thrusting against the silk. "You'd let me love you now?"

"Anytime," she said softly. "Anywhere, any way. Why not? I want you, too, Clancy, and there's no reason you should be uncomfortable when I can fix it so easily." She leaned forward and began unfastening the buttons of his pin-striped shirt. "You should have wakened me earlier."

"Lord, I wish I had," he muttered. He closed his eyes as the tips of her fingers brushed against the naked flesh of his chest. Lisa could see the pulse leap in the hollow of his throat and then drum wildly. She felt a primitive delight that she could bring him so much pleasure. Her fingers tangled in the soft fleece matting his chest and tugged gently. "Clancy, come." She took his big hands and put them on her breasts. Feeling their warmth through the silk she began to tremble. "Love me."

"I do," he said hoarsely. "And I will." His hands contracted on her and she felt herself swell into them. She arched toward him with a little moan. His unsteady hands were pushing aside the blouse and closing on her flesh. A shock of pure desire rocketed through her. She closed her eyes as the tremors started to spread throughout her body.

His thumb and forefinger plucked teasingly at one burgeoning nipple, and he laughed huskily as it hardened and distended to pointed beauty. "Come here, Lisa." The blouse was pushed off her shoulders and the bra followed it. Then she was being lifted to straddle him, his hands running up and down her naked spine in a fever of urgency. He arched her forward and his mouth enveloped her breast with a hungry groan.

Her fingers tangled in his hair and she threw back her head with a silent moan. His tongue on her breast was burning, starting little flames of sensation that touched every part of her body.

"You like that?" he muttered. She couldn't answer: her throat had closed and her breath had stopped in her chest. He took her silence for consent and suckled strongly while his hands rhythmically squeezed her breasts. Finally his lips left her. "I love the taste of you," he murmured. He rubbed his cheek back and forth against her breasts, and she could feel the faint stubble of his beard scraping her softness. It sent a hot liquid tingling to the apex of her thighs. "The feel of you." With each movement his tongue darted out to caress, to tease, to taste. Her hands clenched on his shoulders, her arousal almost unbearable in its intensity. She opened her eyes and watched his lips move against the swollen globes of her breasts, his tongue on her nipples.

Then his hands were on the zipper of her slacks. He didn't lift his head as he slid the zipper down with a soft, sibilant hiss. Then his hands were sliding beneath the waistband, cupping her buttocks. Lisa tensed, the muscles of her stomach knotting painfully. His hands were kneading her feverishly while his lips pulled powerfully at her breast. His chest labored harshly with the force of his breathing, and she could feel the hard length of him pressed against her. She nestled closer with a little moan. His muscles stiffened and his hands dug into her with unconscious force.

She didn't care. The minute pain was only another element in the cascade of sensations. "Don't do that," he said between set teeth. "I'm trying to be gentle, dammit I want everything to be—" He broke off. "Oh, my God. . . ."

"What's the matter?" she whispered.

"The matter is that all my brains seem to be located in my groin," he said with supreme self-disgust. "All I can think about is laying you down across this seat and driving into you."

"Sounds good to me," she said with a faint smile. "It sounds wonderful to me."

His hands tightened on her. "It was a hell of a lot easier to stop when you weren't so willing." His fingers moved yearningly over her skin with tactile hunger. "Say no, Lisa."

"No?" Her eyes widened. "I don't want to say no. Why should I do a stupid thing like that? I'm about to turn into an incendiary bomb and you want me to stop?"

"Please. Say no." His gaze was fastened on the ripe heaviness of her breasts, and he ran his tongue over his lips, remembering the taste of her. "I can't stop unless you do. And it's important to me."

"Why?"

"Because *you're* important to me. All my life sex has been just another appetite to be appeased." He smiled crookedly. "Wham, bam, thank you, ma'am. That's why I automatically behaved like a stud presented with a prize mare when I knew you were going to let me love you. But I don't want that with you. I want it to be special."

Lisa stared at him with a wild mixture of emotions—frustration, desire, exasperation, tenderness. "*Now* you tell me," she said, shaking her head. After a moment her lips began to quirk. "Lord, how I hate a tease." She slid off his lap and into the seat next to him. "All right. I'm saying no. Very reluctantly. But I have an idea you're going to be sorry about this, Clancy."

"I already am." His eyes lingered hungrily on her naked breasts. "You're taking this very well."

"No, I'm not taking it well at all. At the moment I could murder you. Or rape you. I haven't decided which."

He looked startled. "That sounds bawdy, coming from you."

"That's because I am bawdy on occasion." She grinned at him. "Just because I'm a trifle thin and delicate-looking, don't make the mistake of thinking I'm a milk-and-water miss."

He looked at her, his eyes narrowing. "You seem . . . different."

Her smile was a sudden brilliant flash of warmth. "I've come alive. If you don't like it, that's just too bad, Clancy. You're responsible for it."

"I like it," he said softly. "I'm just having a little trouble adjusting to it. I wonder what other surprises I have in store for me." His gaze returned compulsively to her breasts. "Could I persuade you to put on your blouse? Looking at all that lovely bounty is putting me in a very painful state."

She reached down and picked up her blouse,

then slipped it on and began to fasten the pearl buttons.

"Haven't you forgotten something?" He nodded to the lacy scrap of a bra on the seat.

She shook her head and calmly picked up the bra, stuffing it into her tote bag beside the seat. "Nope." She picked up her linen blazer and slipped it on. "I'm taking out insurance."

"Insurance?"

"The way you're behaving is entirely too gallant and noble to suit me. I'm not at all sure how long it's going to take you to set up this 'special' situation in which to make love with me. So I thought I'd add a little incentive. This jacket maintains a façade of respectability, but I want you to know it's only a façade. That I'm naked and available for you." Her smile was both mischievous and wickedly alluring. "That all you have to do is reach out and undo a button or two and you'll have whatever you want. Anytime you want it," she whispered. "Is that enough of a goad to your initiative, Clancy?"

He gave a low whistle. "Why, you little devil. Hell, yes, that's enough of a goad."

"I thought it would be." She leaned forward and began to fasten the buttons on his shirt. Her hands were still trembling, but she didn't try to hide it. She wanted him to see how much she wanted him. She couldn't tell him she loved him as yet, but she could give him that. "Of course, I don't promise to keep *my* hands off you." Demurely, she lowered her lashes to veil her eyes. "But I'll make an effort. It depends on how long you make me wait."

"Well, I promise it won't be long. You're a tough lady to go up against."

She sat back in her seat and picked up a magazine from the table beside her. "But I guarantee you'll enjoy it when you do go up against me," she said softly. "You certainly didn't seem to have any complaints before you got that sudden attack of conscience."

"Lisa, dammit . . ."

She smothered a smile. "Sorry. It's not too late to change your mind about me. You didn't really know what you were getting when you made me that offer. The lady you knew on Paradise Cay was only the tip of the iceberg. Now the part of the iceberg that was submerged is breaking up and bobbing to the surface."

"How does it feel?" he asked, smiling gently.

She thought about it. "Mostly good, I think. Sometimes a bit scary. It's a little difficult to flow with the southern current and feel the ice melting. I can't help wondering what will be left by the time I hit the Equator."

"I know what will be left." His hand reached out and covered hers. "A lady with dignity and character who will have become all she could be. There's nothing to be afraid of in that. I'm looking forward to being around to see it."

Lisa felt a sudden tightness in her throat. Clancy was a rock to cling to in that current. How many other people had used his strength and support in the past? He gave so selflessly that it was easy to forget he had needs as well. She felt a rush of fierce maternal tenderness. Well, she wouldn't forget, and she wouldn't let anyone else forget, either.

She looked blindly down at the magazine on her lap. The moment was so fraught with emotion that she had to lighten it. "I hear that you live in the sheikh's palace. Does that mean I'm going to be established as a harem favorite?"

"You certainly display the erotic temperament for it. I do have quarters at the palace, but that's not where I'm taking you tonight."

Her eyes twinkled. "You're not installing me in a nunnery, by any chance?"

"Not by any possible chance. I have a setting in mind that doesn't lean to either extreme."

"You're not going to tell me where we're going?"

He shook his head. "I want it to be a surprise. I've never planned a romantic tryst before." There was a touch of boyish eagerness in his smile that was very appealing. "I find I'm looking forward to it. I hope to hell I don't mess it up." He stood up and turned toward the cockpit. "It's almost time to land. I'm going to tell John he's to take you sightseeing this afternoon while I complete the arrangements."

She frowned. "But I don't want to go sightseeing. I'd rather stay with you."

He glanced back over his shoulder, his gaze lingering on the unconfined swell of her breasts beneath the silk blouse. Then, with an effort, he averted his eyes. "You should have thought of that before you initiated your little goad, acushla. I wouldn't last five minutes with you in the back of the limousine, and then all my arrangements would go down the drain." He paused. "As it is, I might just last until tonight if I get to the cockpit in the next two seconds." He walked quickly down the aisle.

It wasn't a Middle Eastern palace, but a medieval castle complete with drawbridge, turrets, and a wall to keep out potential invaders. The magnificent anomaly sat squarely in the middle of the Sedikhan desert when it should have occupied a cliff in the British countryside.

"What's the drawbridge for?" Lisa asked blankly. "There's no moat."

The blue-and-white helicopter Clancy was piloting hovered, dipped, and then settled on the flagstones of the courtyard. "The castle was built by one of Lance Rubinoff's more flamboyant ancestors, who decided he was homesick for Tamrovia." His lips curved in a half smile. "He must have been a great deal like Lance, because it apparently didn't make the slightest difference to him that the idea wasn't exactly practical."

"Tamrovia? That's a small monarchy in the Balkans, isn't it?" Clancy had made passing mention of Prince Lance Rubinoff, who was Alex's cousin, but he hadn't gone into any detail. "It's ruled by a King Stefan. I read something about it in *National Geographic*."

Clancy nodded. "Stefan is Lance's older brother. There have been close diplomatic ties between the two countries for decades, but no familial ones until Alex's father married Sheikh Karim's daughter." He turned off the ignition and opened the door of the helicopter. "Lance found the atmosphere at Sedikhan much more to his liking than

Tamrovia and settled here with his wife, Honey. Brother Stefan is a bit of a stuffed shirt, evidently."

And Lance Rubinoff definitely was not. What Lisa had read about him had been in the gossip columns, not the *National Geographic.* He had been the darling of the tabloids with his scandalous love affairs and wild pranks before he was married. Lately his name had appeared more often in the art section as his reputation as an artist had skyrocketed. "This is Lance's castle?"

"No; he uses it occasionally, but it actually belongs to Sedikhan. It was lost to Alex's great-grandfather in a poker game." He lifted her down to the flagstones of the courtyard. "No one is really fond of the old place except Kira, and she's in Tamrovia right now."

"Kira?"

"Princess Kira Rubinoff, Lance's younger sister." He frowned. "Can't we drop the family history bit? I didn't bring you here to regale you with stories of the Rubinoff dynasty."

"Why did you bring me here?" she asked with a teasing grin. "I haven't seen you at all since we arrived in Marasef this afternoon, until John delivered me back at the airport. Then you flew me off in the helicopter to this Ivanhoe's castle. I definitely feel swept off my feet."

"That's how I wanted you to feel," he said quietly, and made a gesture toward the castle. "I thought we'd spend a few months by ourselves before I dropped you into the social whirl in Marasef. Its towers aren't ivory, but I thought it made a fitting background for a princess all the same. I wanted to give you that."

What a touching gesture. Lisa felt tears sting her eyes. "But I don't have the princess mentality anymore. I just want to be a woman." She repeated his own words softly, "A woman with character and dignity."

"I knew I'd blow it. What can you expect when an old war horse like me tries to play Galahad?"

"You *didn't* blow it. It was a beautiful, wonderful thing to do," she said. "I love it. What woman wouldn't want a castle put at her disposal? But I'm afraid I don't deserve it. I'm not sure I can live up to such an extravagant gesture."

"You deserve it." His fingers touched her cheek gently. "And you don't have to have a particularly aristocratic mentality to be a princess." He made a face. "Remind me to introduce you to Kira sometime. What's important is that it gives you pleasure."

"Oh, it does." Impulsively she stood on tiptoe to press a kiss on his cheek. "I can't wait to see the rest of it."

"I'll give you the Cook's tour tomorrow." Clancy took her elbow and propelled her across the courtyard. "Right now, I want to introduce you to Marna and give you a chance to freshen up before dinner."

"Who's Marna?"

"She's the housekeeper of the castle. She used to be Kira's old nurse, and when things got a bit difficult in Tamrovia, Kira whisked her here to Sedikhan."

"Difficult?"

"Just a spot of diplomatic bother involving Kira. Considering that it did involve Kira, it's a wonder it wasn't worse. Marna would probably commit murder to protect her."

Lisa was becoming increasingly intrigued by the casual remarks Clancy dropped regarding Kira Rubinoff. She was clearly a colorful character.

When she was introduced to Marna Debuk a few minutes later, Lisa's curiosity was even more aroused. She couldn't picture anyone "whisking" this woman anywhere. She must have stood six feet tall in her stocking feet, with the deep chest and powerful shoulders of a lady wrestler; the neat, dark dress she wore looked wildly inappropriate. Her face was heavy-jawed, both impassive and ageless, and framed in a helmet of dark hair clipped in a short Dutch bob.

Her large hand completely enveloped Lisa's as they shook hands. The woman murmured a polite acknowledgment in slightly accented English. She turned to Clancy, and for a moment there was a flicker of warmth in her eyes. "Everything's prepared as you instructed, Mr. Donahue. Will you be ready to dine in an hour?"

"That will be fine, Marna. I appreciate your going to all this trouble on such short notice."

"It's no trouble." The housekeeper shrugged. "It gave the servants something to do. No guests have visited here since Kira left a few months ago. They grow lazy."

"I doubt that, with you in charge." Clancy said dryly. "They're all terrified of you."

"Yes." Her dark eyes glinted. "Which is as it should be, as we both know, Mr. Donahue." She turned to Lisa. "If you'll follow me, I'll take you to your room. I hope you will find it suitable. It's the tower room, as Mr. Donahue ordered."

Lisa smothered a smile. Trust Clancy to go all the way. "I'm sure I will." As Marna padded ahead of her down the hall, Lisa cast a quick glance at Clancy. "Aren't you coming?"

He shook his head. "I'll come to your room in an hour and take you down to dinner. I have a few phone calls to make."

A shadow crossed her face. "Martin?"

"Not all my business has to do with Baldwin," Clancy said. "Don't worry, it's too soon for him to surface again. And even if he does, I'll keep you safe."

But would he be able to keep himself safe? Martin had been so chillingly malignant that day in the market. Lisa gave herself an admonishing shake. She wouldn't think about unhappy things tonight. Tonight was very special. "I know you will." She smiled at him. "And you can bet I'll wait for you to come and get me. This place is absolutely huge. I might get lost and never be heard of again. How many rooms does this castle have, for goodness' sake?"

"Thirty-two, excluding the servants' quarters."

"Oh, my, when you furnish a lady with a castle, you do it right, Clancy. I'd better get moving or I may lose my guide." She waved and hurried after Marna.

He watched her as she climbed the wide stone steps of the staircase in the foyer. She moved quickly, her carriage light and graceful, her delicate coloring contrasting sharply with the harsh gray of the stone wall.

He felt a swift rush of possessiveness that was as powerful as it was sudden. Tonight she was going to belong to him. If he was lucky, that one night might possibly turn into forever. When she disappeared from view, he turned and walked across the hall to the library. It took him only a few minutes to get through to Galbraith in Marasef. "Is there any word yet?"

"Not even a whisper. I called Berthold and told him to keep an eye out in case Baldwin returned to the island, and also contacted our operatives in the U.S. and alerted them." Galbraith paused. "But you don't really think he'll return to either place, do you?"

"No. I think he'll go to Said Ababa and join his terrorist friends. He knows he'll be safe there." Clancy's tone roughened. "And with their contacts in Sedikhan, he won't find it difficult to discover where Lisa can be found. It's a combination he'll find hard to resist."

"Then hadn't you better return to Marasef? You're pretty isolated out there in the desert."

"On the contrary, in the starkness of the desert you notice anything unusual at once. I can't say the same about a crowded city like Marasef. I want you to send a few of our best men out here tomorrow. Tell them they'll pose as servants. I don't want Lisa worrying about all this."

"You'll be staying out there indefinitely?"

"Until we get Baldwin." There was a slightly sardonic note in Clancy's voice as he added, "It would be nice if you made the effort to capture him before we have to confront him here. If it's not too much bother."

"Testy, aren't we?" Galbraith asked lightly. "I'll do everything short of crossing the Said Ababa border. Okay?"

"Okay, and for God's sake keep in touch."

Clancy hung up the receiver and stared at it abstractedly for a moment. He had been a little testy. He knew Galbraith would do everything possible to capture Baldwin if he crossed the border. It was just that he was so damned scared for Lisa.

He checked his watch and then moved swiftly to the door. Fifteen minutes had already passed, and he wanted to shower and change before he joined her. An elegant tuxedo wouldn't turn him into the kind of glamorous knight a princess deserved, but by God, he could try.

Seven

To Lisa's relief, dinner was served in a small oval dining room instead of the high-ceilinged hall she had glimpsed from the foyer. The walls were hung with rich tapestries faded with age and lit with flickering candles in a silver candelabra. The oak table was also oval and gleamed in the candlelight with an age-silkened patina. The entire castle had an air of dignity and grace, reminiscent of a bygone time, she mused. Though the modern comforts of electricity and efficient plumbing had been added, they hadn't been allowed to interfere with the ambience of the place.

The maid who served them was quick and deft and appeared a little nervous as she moved around the table serving the delicious duck à l'orange. When a tiny drop of sauce dropped on Lisa's placemat, she gasped with horror, her gaze flying

125

to the figure of Marna Debuk standing unobtrusively just to the left of the doorway. Marna frowned. The girl gasped again and hurried from the room.

"What was that all about?" Lisa asked.

"It was nothing," Marna said with a shrug. "I'm sorry the foolish girl was so clumsy. I will send in another maid from the kitchen." She left the room, moving with surprising grace for a woman of her bulk.

Lisa met Clancy's eyes across the table, and she grinned in amusement. "And I thought the headwaiter at the cafe was intimidating. I don't believe I ever saw any of the waiters blanch and run from the room when Monty frowned."

"But Monty wasn't a gypsy believed to be able to cast spells and hexes," Clancy said dryly. "His subordinates only have to worry about their jobs."

"She's a gypsy?"

"A genuine, card-carrying gypsy," Clancy said with a grin. "There are several tribes in Tamrovia that travel in caravans around the countryside. She belongs to one of the more powerful ones."

"But how did a gypsy become nursemaid to a royal princess?"

"Tradition. In olden times it was believed that gypsies had great magical powers, and to have one in attendance on their children was a social coup. It became a custom in Marna's tribe to send a chosen one to serve in the royal household in every generation. Unfortunately, Their Majesties made the mistake of assigning Marna to Kira when she was born."

"Why unfortunately?"

"Because combining a lawless gypsy philosophy like Marna's with Kira's temperament was like adding oil to fire." He picked up his glass of wine. "Explosive."

"Fascinating," Lisa murmured.

"If you like to play with dynamite." He smiled. "Personally I like my entertainment a little less volatile. Have I told you how lovely you look tonight? I like that caftan."

"So do I." She touched the peach-colored brocade of the bodice. She knew the color was good with her hair and eyes, and the richness of the material always made her feel festive. "Though the style is more fitting to one of your Middle Eastern palaces than this castle."

"Oh, I don't know. I imagine quite a few knights brought their ladies gorgeous garb like that from their crusades."

"I hadn't thought of that." She wasn't thinking very coherently of anything, she thought ruefully. Her palms were actually damp with nervousness. Good Lord, she was acting with all the sophistication of a teenage virgin. She should have seduced Clancy this afternoon on the plane. Then she had responded with complete naturalness and passion. Now that she'd had time to think how important tonight might be to her, she had developed a case of nerves.

"You're not eating again." Clancy's eyes were twinkling. "You mustn't disappoint Marna. She might put the evil eye on you."

"Is that why you brought me here? So that Marna could accomplish what you and Galbraith couldn't?"

He went still. "You know why I brought you here," he said quietly. "And it has nothing to do with that particular appetite."

Her chest was suddenly so tight she was finding it hard to breathe. She could see the reflection of the candle flames in his eyes, but she doubted if that was what made them blaze. The room was charged with an electricity and naked desire that was unmistakable. Why were they sitting here indulging in this charade of social amenities when neither of them wanted to be anywhere but in each other's arms? She swallowed. "You don't seem to be eating very well yourself. Shall we give it up and take the risk of incurring Marna's wrath?"

He threw the napkin on the table and stood up. "If we can manage to escape before she comes back from the kitchen." He was around the table, pulling her to her feet. "Let's go!"

They ran from the room like naughty children, only to be confronted by Marna in the hall. Braking, they skidded to a stop.

"You do not wish dessert?" the housekeeper asked, raising a brow.

Clancy shook his head. "Miss Landon needs some fresh air. We thought we'd take a walk on the battlements."

The faintest smile touched Marna's lips. "It is always wise to satisfy one's needs when they occur. It is unhealthy to do otherwise. Good night, Mr. Donahue."

Lisa stared after her retreating figure. "Maybe she is a witch. That had to be a double entendre."

"She wouldn't have to be psychic to read our minds at the moment. There's a certain look. . . ."

He grinned. "Though I wouldn't swear that she didn't." He took her hand and pulled her up the stairs. When they reached the landing he suddenly turned to her with a frown. "Would you like to?"

She blinked. "What?"

"See the battlements. I don't want you to think I'm rushing you off to the sack. And I suppose a stroll in the moonlight would be romantic."

She gazed at him with exasperation and enormous tenderness. "Clancy, you've done your duty. You've provided me with all the romance a woman could possibly want. Now for God's sake, will you take me to *bed*?"

A slow smile lit his face. "Did I ever tell you how much I admire an aggressive woman? You're damn right I will."

He rushed her up the second flight of stairs with a speed that had her choking with laughter. Then he swung her up in his arms and strode down the hall. "One last romantic gesture. I was tempted to carry you up the stairs like Rhett Butler did Scarlett, but I thought you'd prefer to have me able to function when we got to the top."

He opened the door of a room at the end of the corridor and carried her into a large bedroom much like her own. Several crystal candelabra bearing long white tapers were scattered about the room, and the flames cast dancing shadows on the walls. Lisa was vaguely aware of tapestries in muted hues covering those walls, Aubusson area rugs on the stone floors, and a huge canopied four-poster bed across the room.

"Romance isn't everything." He set her on her feet and kicked the door shut behind him. "In a situation like this, stamina counts for a hell of a lot, too."

"Clancy . . ." She gazed up at him helplessly. Why didn't he realize how wonderful he was? "Don't you know you don't have to act romantic? You *are* romantic. You're handsome, brave, and intelligent."

"And sexy?" he suggested solemnly.

"And sexy." She nodded. "Oh, yes, very sexy."

"Just testing. I wanted to be sure you appreciated all my attributes." Suddenly he put his arms around her and buried his face in her hair. "Oh, God, I didn't think I'd ever make it." His hands moved feverishly on her back. His lips were on her ear, her temple, her cheek in soft, hot kisses. "It seems as if I've been aching for this for at least a decade or so."

Lisa could feel the hardness of his rigid muscles against her, but he wasn't close enough. She cuddled nearer, rotating in a sinuous little movement into the cradle of his hips. He inhaled sharply. His heart was pounding so hard she could detect the movement through his white dress shirt.

His tongue darted in her ear and she moaned deep in her throat, arching against him as if he'd jerked a hidden string.

"Naked," he muttered. "I've got to get you naked." His unsteady hands were unfastening the barrette that held back her hair and then combing through the loosened tresses until they fell in a shimmering cloud down her back.

"Clancy, that barrette wasn't exactly a significant body covering." Lia laughed shakily. "If you'll let me go for a minute, I'll see if I can improve on what you started."

His hips moved slowly against her, rotating, stroking her sensuously, his hands cupping her buttocks to bring her in closer contact. Their lower bodies were pressed so close that she could feel the heat of his arousal with every breath. "I don't want to let you go," he said. She could hear his ragged breathing as he pressed his fevered cheek against her temple. Then he was pushing her away. "Quick. For God's sake, be quick."

He didn't need to urge her to speed. When he had pushed her away she'd felt an aching sense of loss, as if they had been joined and were now severed by a surgeon's scalpel. She *needed* that joining.

She moved swiftly, pulling the caftan over her head and then dispensing with her slippers and underthings with equal speed. Then she was back in his arms and was aware of the shock of naked flesh against her own. Clancy had stripped with the same frantic urgency she had.

"Clancy . . ." Her fingers dug into his shoulders as she rubbed her body against him with exquisite sensuous pleasure.

The cloud of hair on his chest was teasing her sensitive breasts, the hard muscles and bones of his thighs were locked and rigid with a leashed threat that was deliciously exciting. With every movement of her body he gave a little gasp that was almost a groan. She was gasping, too. Each breath was a shock of sensation as it brought her flesh in fresh contact with his. His left thigh insinuated itself between hers, and she could feel the thick muscles, lightly dusted with hair, pressing against her softness.

Her teeth clenched to suppress a cry that could well have turned into a scream. Heat. Wanting. His thigh moved with soft abrasiveness against her womanhood in an urgent, mindless rhythm that was making her mindless as well. "No more," she whispered. "No more, Clancy."

He nodded jerkily. "No more," he agreed. His chest was heaving with the force of his breathing. "Come on." He half pulled her across the room to the bed. Once there, he didn't wait to jerk down the spread but pushed her down on the cool satin surface. His eyes were glazed and almost blind as he followed her down and settled himself between her thighs. "Are you ready for me? I hope to heaven you're ready." He didn't wait for an answer but plunged deep with a low groan that was almost painful. Fire, fullness, hunger. So much hunger surrounded them. She felt it in him even as he took, feasted, filled. Her own hunger, too, seemed completely insatiable.

She arched upward helplessly as he thrust with a force and passion that sent shudder after shudder through her body. Hot, slick, driving. Her nails dug into his shoulders with unconscious force. His face above her was heavy with the same hunger and a pleasure that was primitive and exciting as the act itself. The muscles of his torso were strained with unbearable tension.

She didn't know how long that mindless rapture continued. The tension mounted constantly, spiraling, sparking, until she didn't think she could stand it for one more minute. Her head thrashed back and forth on the satin spread, her hair splaying in wild abandon. She *felt* abandoned and wild and . . .

He was moving more forcefully within her. Plunging, rotating, thrusting deeper when she hadn't thought there was a deeper. A cry escaped from her as the tension broke and then splintered into a thousand sharp, glittering prisms of splendor.

She heard a low, harsh groan above her that sounded as if it had been torn from him, and then she was caught close to Clancy's big body. Her arms closed around him fiercely, protectively, with a loving possession that she had never known before. *She* had brought him this wild, mindless pleasure. It had been her body that had assuaged his hunger and then made him tremble with satisfaction. That knowledge was almost as wonderful as the passionate glory that had gone before.

His heart was slowing now, though his chest was still laboring with the force of his breathing.

"Lisa . . ." His voice was oddly choked. "Lord, I'm sorry."

Shock jolted through the euphoria she was feeling. "Sorry? Why on earth are you sorry?"

"You know why," he said with self-disgust as he shifted off her to one side. "I did just what I said I wouldn't do. Wham, bam, thank you, ma'am. Just as if you were some call girl I'd ordered for a one-night stand."

Oh, dear, if Clancy didn't get over these romantic illusions of what she was due as his lady, they were going to have a difficult time of it. She sat up and brushed the hair from her face, then turned to look at him. "Do you know what a truly romantic man does, Clancy? He gives a woman what she wants." She grinned down at him. "And I assure you, that's exactly what you did just now. I wanted wham and bam, and a sincerely expressed thank-you wouldn't be far off the mark, either. I certainly feel fervently grateful to you." Her voice lowered to a whisper of tenderness. "It was beautiful. Thank you, Clancy Donahue."

He looked at her searchingly, then pulled her down to kiss her with an exquisite sweetness that caused her throat to tighten with tears. "You're welcome," he said gruffly, then fell silent again. "There aren't any words, you know. What happened was . . ." He shrugged helplessly and repeated, "There just aren't any words."

"Then don't try to say them." She cuddled closer, nestling her head in the hollow of his shoulder, her fingers tangling contentedly in the crisp hair on his chest. "You certainly don't need them. You do extremely well with body language."

His chuckle reverberated beneath her ear. "I'll remember which form of communication you prefer." His lips feathered a kiss on the top of her head. "Nap a little, love, and then we'll see if we can develop a few new innovations to the state of the art."

There was the lightest brushing at the crests of her breasts, then a warm, wet teasing and probing, and then a tugging. It was all deliciously gentle and lazy and right. Sleepily Lisa opened her eyes to see Clancy's dark head nestled at her breasts, and she smiled with contentment.

His head lifted and he smiled, too. "Hi," he said softly. His hand moved to cup the swelling globe that had been receiving his attention. "Did I ever tell you that you have fantastic breasts?"

"I don't believe the subject has come up, but I'm glad one part of my anatomy meets with your approval. All I've been hearing lately is how skinny I am."

"Well, these lovely things are definitely *not* skinny." His tongue placed another caress on the rosy peak. His hand ran down her midriff to her belly, and he began to massage it gently. "Your hips are damned narrow, though, and you're awfully tiny here." He frowned. "You won't have trouble with the baby, will you?"

She stiffened in surprise. She had completely forgotten that this heady delight also had a purpose. She might have a child as the result of this night. A quiet glow of joy swept over her. "I didn't with Tommy. It's the pelvis measurements that count."

He was still frowning as his hand moved down to press the tight curls at the apex of her thighs. "I'm so blasted big. Our child is bound to be—"

She reached down and covered his lips with her hand. "Hush, it will be fine. Let me worry about the actual production process. You just keep your mind on your part of the project."

His lips parted and he nipped at the fingers covering them. "That won't be hard to do. I'm having trouble keeping my mind on anything else when you're around." Suddenly his cheek was on her stomach, rubbing back and forth with loving affection. She could feel the slight roughness of his beard growth against her smoothness. It brought a sudden hot tingling sensation between her thighs that sent a ripple of surprise through her. So soon? His words were slightly muffled. "You're not sorry? You haven't changed your mind?"

"It's a little late for second thoughts." Her hand tangled in the thickness of his hair. "No, I'm not sorry. It was wonderful, Clancy."

His lips caressed her. "For me, too. I think it's very convenient that baby making is so damn enjoyable. I intend to work very hard on the project, you realize." His fingers wandered between her thighs and began stroking her lazily. "Morning, noon, and night." She gasped as his fingers suddenly plunged forward. "And in between, of course."

"What about your job?" she asked faintly. He was moving lazily, rhythmically within her, and her back arched helplessly.

"I can take a little vacation. I feel it's my duty to devote all my energies to this project at the present time." Unexpectedly, he was over her, entering her with one powerful movement. "There are certain priorities I have to keep in mind." He looked down at her and the lazy humor faded. In addition to the heavy sensuality she had expected, there was a gravity that surprised her. "And you're my top priority, Lisa." He leaned down and kissed her gently. "Always."

Then he started to move and she forgot everything but the web of passion he was weaving about her.

*   *   *

"Where are you going?"

Lisa settled the caftan around her hips and slipped on her shoes. "I didn't mean to wake you. I just thought I'd go back to my room and shower and change before breakfast. I wasn't exactly prepared when you decided to sweep me off my feet and into bed." She winked. "At last."

"You should have been. I was aiming at being a romantic, not a complete idiot." He crossed his arms under his head and leaned lazily back on the pillow. "But now I've decided to become a satyr instead. I've discovered I'm suited for it both psychologically and physically. Come back to bed, Lisa. I need some practice in the role."

She lifted a slightly derisive brow. "After last night?" Neither of them had counted the times they'd come together in a passion that had seemed unquenchable. Even now she was tempted to do as he asked and go back into his arms. "After breakfast we'll discuss it again. I wouldn't want you to dwindle down to a mere shadow." She crossed the room and opened the door. "I'll meet you in the dining room in an hour." She started to close the door, then stopped in surprise. "What the devil is this?" She held up a small leather drawstring pouch. "I found it hanging on the doorknob."

Clancy took one look at the pouch and a smile tugged at his lips. "Marna. It's a charm of some sort. I've seen them hanging on Kira's doorknobs on occasion."

Lisa lifted the pouch to her nose and sniffed experimentally. "Well, it doesn't smell of garlic, so evidently we're not threatened by vampires. I wonder what it could be."

"There's no telling. Why don't you go ask her? I was going to call Alex before breakfast anyway."

"Do you think I should? After all, it was hanging on your doorknob. She might tell me it's none of my business."

"I doubt that. Marna has an uncanny way of knowing what's going on around her. I'm sure she knows you were occupying this room last night." His expression grew sober. "Not only last night, I hope. I know it's not considered chic for a couple to occupy the same bedroom these days, but I'd like very much to have you move in with me." Gruffly he added, "I'll try not to get in your way."

"I'd like that, too," she said. "I'll pack and move my things from my room right after breakfast."

"You won't miss your tower, princess? I hate to be an Indian giver. You occcupied that room for less than an hour."

"Not a bit. I've decided that towers are too lonely for me, anyway." She blew him a kiss and closed the door.

Her step was as springy and light as her mood as she strolled down the corridor. Now if she could only manage to find her room in this labyrinth, it would make her day. She hadn't been paying any attention to where they were going last night when Clancy had been playing Rhett Butler. For that matter, she hadn't noticed anything but Clancy.

Lisa only lost her way once in the twisting corridors before she found the right wing. Next time she ventured in this area, she told herself, she'd have to leave a trail of bread crumbs like those children in the fairy tale. However, Marna would probably not appreciate bread crumbs in her immaculate halls, she thought ruefully. The gypsy housekeeper would soon be putting a pouch on her doorknob to attract vampires instead of keeping them away.

She opened the door to her room and went directly to the closet to get a robe. She stood stock still, a puzzled frown creasing her brow. The closet was almost empty. There was a terry-cloth robe, a blouse, and a pair of slacks on the padded hangers. What had happened to the rest of her clothes? She had unpacked and hung up everything last night before she'd dressed for dinner.

She slipped the robe from the hanger and crossed to the bureau. One set of underwear remained in the middle drawer. Everything else was gone. In the adjoining bathroom her makeup and toiletries remained on the vanity. Whoever had removed her belongings had been very selective. Marna? Lisa doubted if any of the maids would have dared touch her things without Marna's approval; she clearly had them all under her control. It was evident there was something to discuss with the housekeeper besides the talisman.

After Lisa had showered and dressed, she set out to try to locate Marna for that discussion. Finally she tracked the housekeeper down in the kitchen, which proved to be a converted scullery in the cellars of the castle. Marna was standing beside a modernistic microwave oven, consulting in a low voice with a white-clad boy.

She turned an expressionless face as Lisa approached her. "Breakfast will be served in twenty minutes. You wish something special?"

"No, anything will be fine. I just—"

"This is Hassan, Miss Landon." She gave the boy a surprisingly warm smile. "He is the cook. He was responsible for your dinner last night."

"It was a wonderful dinner, Hassan. We enjoyed it very much." She turned to the housekeeper. "I wonder if I could speak to you for a moment, Miss Debuk."

"Marna," she corrected as she turned away from the stove. "I'm through here, we can go upstairs now." She gave the cook another fleeting smile and led the way through the scullery and up the curving stone steps to the hall. "Hassan is a good boy with sense in his head. Not like those other *chitkas.*"

"*Chitkas?*"

"Fools. It is a Tamrovian word. They fear everything they don't understand."

"Well, there's a few things I don't understand that I'd appreciate your explaining."

"But you are not afraid to ask. Those *chitkas* run away and hide instead of asking. I have no use for them. You remember that clumsy girl who served you dinner last night?" When Lisa nodded she went on with a scowl, "Lia ran away last night before I could even talk to her. She left a message that she was returning to her village and would not be back. Now why would she do that?"

"She seemed to be afraid of your disapproval." Lisa paused. "And I got the distinct impression that you enjoyed the image you were projecting."

There was a flicker of grudging respect in Marna's dark eyes. "I do," she said with a shrug. "I grow bored with these *chitkas.* If they fear, why shouldn't I feed it a little?" She frowned. "But not that much. Lia makes good wages here and she needs the work. I'll have to go to the village and bring her back this morning."

It appeared there was a soft streak beneath that fierce exterior. "Could you answer a few questions before you go running after her?"

Marna looked at her without expression. "Of course. What would you like to know? Should I get my tarot cards?"

Lisa could feel her lips gape in surprise. Merciful heaven, the woman did believe she had psychic powers!

"No, I don't think that will be necessary. You won't need a crystal ball to answer this one. Where are my clothes?"

"They should be in Mr. Donahue's room by now. Last night I had a maid take them downstairs to press and freshen them a little. She was told to take them to Mr. Donahue's room this morning and put them away." She frowned. "You must tell me if she hasn't done it properly. She is a *chitka*, too."

That appeared to be the woman's favorite word, Lisa thought. "But why would you do that?"

"You wish to occupy Mr. Donahue's bed and his room," Marna said simply. "And Mr. Donahue wishes you to be there. There was no need for you to pack yourself. I took care of it for you."

"But how did you—" Lisa broke off, totally bewildered. The question of the change of rooms hadn't even come up before this morning, and Marna had put the wheels in motion last night.

"You did want to move?"

"Yes, but—"

"Good. I will send the girl for the few things that were left in the tower chamber at once." Marna turned back toward the scullery. "It is good that you do this. Mr. Donahue is a *disek*. He will have a fine strong son."

"*Disek?*" Lisa repeated numbly. She felt as if she'd been caught in the middle of a tornado.

"A *disek* is one of the exceptional ones, an individual with power and strength," Marna said. "Did he tell you that he helped Kira when she was trying to smuggle me out of Tamrovia?"

"No, he didn't tell me that."

Marna nodded. "That *chitka*, Stefan, thought he would gain the upper hand, but Kira and Mr. Donahue fooled him."

"King Stefan?" It appeared that nervous servants weren't the only *chitkas* in Marna's estimation.

"Kira's brother," Marna confirmed, nodding.

"Stefan is not a *disek*?"

Marna shook her head emphatically. "A *chitka*."

"I see." She didn't, but she was afraid to increase her confusion by delving any deeper. "Then you must be very grateful to Clancy for his help."

"Of course. Why do you think I made the *nathal* and hung it on his doorknob?"

Nathal. Lisa reached into the pocket of her slacks and pulled out the small pouch. "This is a *nathal*?"

Marna nodded with satisfaction. "The most powerful *nathal* I have ever made."

"Just precisely what does a *nathal* do?" Lisa asked warily.

"Why, what you wished it to do." She turned and crossed back to where Lisa was standing. "May I touch you?"

Lisa nodded, puzzled.

Marna put her large hand gently on Lisa's abdomen and closed her eyes. It was only for the briefest instant, and then her hand was gone and she turned away. "Yes, there was no problem. I thought not. It was a very strong *nathal*."

"You didn't answer me," Lisa said, exasperated and close to desperate. "What does a *nathal* do?"

"It is a fertility talisman," Marna said calmly as she glided down the hall. "You both wished for a child, and now you have it. A fine son who will grow into a *disek* like his father." She glanced over her shoulder. "But you must eat more than you did last night from now on. It is not good for the child for you to be so thin."

Lisa watched as the door closed behind her. Good heavens, now Marna was nagging her about eating, too, she thought half-hysterically. Would the woman make a charm to increase her appetite if she wasn't satisfied? Oh, Lord, the whole thing was crazy. Yet there had been something so serenely confident in Marna's last statement. And how had she known they wanted a child?

She shook her head to clear it, but it did little good. She still felt as if she'd been transported back to fantasyland.

"What's wrong?" She turned to see Clancy coming out of the library down the hall. "Don't you feel well?"

"I don't know. I've just been talking to Marna. I don't know which side is up at the moment."

A little smile tugged at Clancy's lips. "I should have known. It's not an unusual reaction. Did you find out what the talisman is for?"

She nodded. "It appears you don't have to work so hard on our little project after all. Marna has fixed everything." She held up the pouch. "Fertility talisman."

Clancy chuckled. "I suspected as much."

"Well, why didn't you tell me?" Lisa demanded.

"Because, my love, Marna can't be explained. She has to be experienced. I thought this was the quickest way for you to do that."

"I certainly 'experienced' her all right. Heavens, the woman is strange." She hesitated. "What do you think? Is there anything to this talisman stuff?" She put her hand to her head and groaned. "Just listen to me; she's got me half believing it. I must be as strange as she is."

Clancy's expression was thoughtful. "I've lived long enough that I don't discount the possibility that powers like that exist, and I've seen Marna do some very impressive hocus-pocus. Who knows?"

Lisa unconsciously touched her abdomen where Marna's hand had rested only a short time ago. Was it possible that the woman was right and even now the seed of a child was growing within her? "A son," she said softly.

"What?"

"Marna said the talisman had worked and I was carrying your son."

He went still. There was an expression on his face so beautiful that she wanted to remember it forever.

"She may be wrong," Lisa whispered. "How could she know?"

He crossed the few paces between them, then reached out and lifted her chin so that he could look into her eyes. His own still held such wonder that she felt her throat tighten with emotion. Then he kissed her with exquisite gentleness. "Well, we certainly won't stop trying. It's far too enjoyable an exercise." He laughed huskily. "I think, if anything, we should redouble our efforts. As you said, how could she know?"

He kissed her again and turned her toward the small room where they had dined last night. "Breakfast," he said firmly. "And it wouldn't hurt you to try to eat a little more. Just in case she's right."

"That's what Marna told me," Lisa said with a sigh. "I'm glad Galbraith's not here. At least I only have the two of you to contend with."

"You'll find that quite enough, acushla."

Lisa nodded gloomily as she allowed him to propel her toward the dining room. She had an idea that withstanding the machinations of a protective gypsy witch and a possessive Clancy Donahue would be more than enough of a challenge for any woman.

Eight

"Milk again." Lisa glared balefully at the frosty glass on the tray Marna was carrying. "I told Lia I didn't want it."

"That is why I brought it back, instead of sending her," Marna said calmly. "It wasn't fair to send the girl all the way back up here to the battlements when you're being so unreasonable. You know you must have it." She held out the wide-brimmed straw hat she had in her other hand. "This, also. The sunlight and fresh air are good for you, but you must have protection."

Lisa took the hat. "I don't like milk," she said. "I'm taking every possible pill under the sun. Iron, vitamins, calcium. I don't need milk, too." She looked down at the swell of her belly beneath the loose tunic top. "He's probably already got vitamin burnout." She had done it again: Marna persistently referred to the baby in the masculine pronoun, and she had picked it up as well.

"The doctor said that milk would—"

"Oh, all right." Lisa jammed the hat on her head, then reached for the milk and drank it down chug-a-lug. Then she put the glass back on the tray. "Satisfied?"

Marna nodded. "You shouldn't be so cross. It's bad—"

"For the baby," Lisa finished wearily. "I know, Marna." She was usually more tolerant of this incessant hovering, but her nerves were on edge today. She wasn't used to Clancy being away. In the last four and a half months he hadn't stirred from the castle for more than a half day's trip to Marasef.

When Alex had called Clancy yesterday morning and summoned him to the capital, she had been as disappointed as if Clancy were going away for a month instead of only one night. That was one of the reasons she'd come up here on the battlements to sunbathe. She could see everything for miles around from this falcon's perch, and she would be sure to spot Clancy's helicopter as soon as it came over the horizon.

She supposed it was childish to be so eager. Martin had gone away for months at a time and she'd never felt this sense of loss. But then she'd never really been in love before. Sometimes it was so strong that she couldn't believe it. Now it appeared impossible that she had been afraid her love for Clancy might not last. The tenderness and passion she felt for him now dwarfed the emotion she had known the night she'd made her decision.

She didn't know why she hadn't told him how much he meant to her. No, that wasn't true; she mustn't be dishonest with herself. She did know: she was terribly frightened. She loved him as much as she had Tommy, and Tommy had been taken from her. Every time she thought about the same thing happening to Clancy, the panic rose to terrifying proportions. She had an irrational feeling that if she didn't say the words, it would keep him safe. What the gods didn't know, they couldn't destroy. Each time she would try to tell Clancy, the panic would rise until it overwhelmed her. Heavens, she was becoming as superstitious as Marna. She would tell Clancy soon how she felt. Surely that stupid fear would disappear when she had had time to get accustomed to loving him so much.

Lisa smiled. "I'm sorry, Marna. You're right. I'm being a shrew. It's just that I wanted to go with Mr. Donahue." She held up her hand as Marna pursed her lips. "I know what the doctor said about being careful for the next month or so. I don't know why I'm having trouble with this pregnancy. My first one was as smooth as silk."

"You are older now."

She made a face. "Thanks a lot." It was true giving birth had a tendency to be a little more difficult at her age. Yet it had surprised as well as frightened her when she had almost lost the baby in the second month. She didn't feel any older than when she carried Tommy. She felt younger and vibrantly, wonderfully alive.

"Mr. Donahue was right. It was best you stay

here and rest." Marna frowned. "Though climbing up all these steps to the battlements is not rest, either."

"I'm very careful and take my time. I wouldn't do anything to risk the baby." Her hand unconsciously went to her belly. She was carrying the child squarely in the front, as she had with Tommy, and was going to be just as large. She had been feeling terribly unattractive lately, and that might have contributed to her depression when Clancy had flown into Marasef without her.

At the palace Clancy would probably run into any number of beautiful, *slim* women, she thought gloomily. When he came back he would probably take one look at her and make an excuse to return. Most men had a chance to appreciate their women's trim figures for some time before this change came about. She had cheated Clancy by blowing up like a balloon only a few months after he had set eyes on her. He'd never said a word about her increasing bulk, but that didn't mean anything. Clancy was always gentle and tactful with her.

A faint whirring broke her reverie and she sat up eagerly in the chair. Her hand reached up to shade her eyes, and she exclaimed with satisfaction. Marna's gaze followed hers to the helicopter just appearing on the horizon. She frowned and then slowly shook her head. "No, it's not Mr. Donahue."

"Of course it is. I recognize the helicopter." Lisa was already on her feet and hurrying toward the door that led to the stairs. "I'll go meet him in the courtyard."

"It's not . . ." Marna stopped. Lisa had already disappeared. She turned back to watch the approaching helicopter. A smile that held an element of fierce joy curved her lips. "Kira."

The wind stirred by the propellers of the helicopter whipped Lisa's tunic against her body as it settled on the flagstones of the courtyard. She took an eager step forward, then stopped as her heart gave a sickening lurch of disappointment. Marna was right; it wasn't Clancy piloting the helicopter. The door opened and an auburn head emerged from the cockpit.

"Hi, I'm Kira Rubinoff." The petite pilot jumped to the ground and slammed the door of the helicopter. "You must be Lisa. Sorry to barge in here without an invitation, but Clancy said it would be all right. I wanted to see Marna." She smiled engagingly. "Not that I wasn't curious about you, too. Clancy has been keeping you to himself for so long that we're all wild to meet you."

"All?"

"Lance and Alex and . . ." She shrugged. "Oh, just everybody. Everyone loves Clancy, and we wanted to make sure you were good enough for—" She broke off with a grimace. "Oh, Lord, there I go again. I don't know why Stefan thinks I'd ever be even a mediocre queen. With my lack of diplomacy, there's every chance I'd start World War Three."

She crossed to Lisa and held out a small, well-shaped hand. "If Clancy chose you, I'm sure you're wonderful. Please forgive me."

How could she do anything else? Lisa thought. The girl had a zestful, exuberant charm that was completely irresistible. Kira Rubinoff couldn't have been more than twenty-two, but she had a poise and presence far beyond her years. She was only a little over five feet, and every one of those inches was curvaceous and alluring. Even in faded jeans and a white T-shirt she exuded a potent sex appeal—a good deal of which was probably generated by a head of flaming auburn hair that tumbled to her shoulders in a riot of curls. The face framed by that shining mass was more intriguing than pretty. High cheekbones, beautifully curved lips that held a hint of sensitivity, and deep sapphire eyes that were slightly tilted.

"I'm very glad to meet you, Princess Rubinoff." Lisa took her hand. "And I'm *not* good enough for Clancy. But then I don't think anyone would be. I do try, however."

"Kira. I've been Princess Rubinoff for the last three months and it's practically driven me bananas. Please don't remind me."

"That's Clancy's helicopter, isn't it? Why didn't he come with you?"

"Something hot is breaking in Marasef with the terrorist situation, and he had to stay longer. He said to tell you he'd be in late tonight or early tomorrow morning."

Lisa felt a chill run through her. "Terrorists?"

"He's not in any danger," Kira said quickly. "They've just heard some of the group have crossed the border from Said Ababa, and they're trying to round up informers to find out where they're hiding." She smiled and suddenly her face was vividly alive. "We'll have a chance to get to know each other. You're an American, aren't you? I went to school in the U.S. Yale. Stefan wanted me to go to the Sorbonne, but I convinced him that I was very impressed by the Communist activities there, so he changed his mind."

Lisa raised a brow. "And were you interested in the Communists?"

"Of course not. I have no idea whether there are any Communists at the Sorbonne. But that was the only way I could get him to send me to America." Her eyes twinkled. "He wasn't about to risk nurturing a Communist sympathizer who might overthrow the monarchy. He may be a bit thick, but he has heard about the Russian Revolution."

"I can see how he might object," Lisa said, smiling.

Kira shrugged. "Oh, Stefan objects to everything about me. He believes that I was born solely to initiate havoc and disturb the peace."

"And have you been doing that?"

It was Marna's deep voice behind them, and Kira whirled with a little cry. Then the girl flew across the courtyard and into her arms. "Oh, Marna, I missed you so." The poise and sophistication were suddenly gone, and she looked like a little girl as she was enfolded in the large woman's embrace. "I tried so hard to be good, but he kept bringing out these horribly depressing types with sweaty palms and brains the size of peas."

"You shouldn't have gone back. I told you it would do no good." Marna stroked Kira's fiery hair with amazing tenderness. "What happened this time?"

"I was too impatient. It had been three months and my being good hadn't seemed to make any difference. We were at the country estate and Stefan was showing everyone through the stables. He'd just bought that prize jumper from the Calumet stables and Don Esteban—"

"Don Esteban is one of these sweaty palm types?" Marna interrupted.

Kira nodded. "The very clammiest, and he kept putting them on me. I couldn't stand him. He was always bragging about his prowess in the bullring. It appears the big wine tycoon is an amateur bull-fighter. You know how I hate bullfights. Those poor bulls . . ."

"I know," Marna said quietly.

"Well, we were passing by this empty stall and his hand just happened to fall on my derriere." She shrugged. "So I tripped him and he fell into the stall."

"Is that all?"

"That was enough. The stableboys hadn't cleaned it out yet, and that wasn't all he fell into." Kira made a face. "Stefan was watching and he was absolutely furious." She nestled closer. "So I hopped a plane and flew back to Marasef. I thought I'd give him time to cool off before I went back."

"You're not going back," Marna said harshly. "It is useless. Why should you let that *chitka* make you unhappy?"

"You know why. I'm not going—" Suddenly she broke off and turned to face Lisa. "Lord, I'm sorry. We're being terribly rude. You must be awfully bewildered by all of this."

"It's none of my business," Lisa said. "If you'd rather be alone . . ."

Kira shook her head. "Clancy cares about you

and he helped us when we needed it." She shrugged. "Heaven knows it's no big secret. The entire family know why we're in Sedikhan." She glanced at Lisa's protruding stomach, and a flicker of mischief lit her eyes. "Clancy's obviously been too busy to fill you in—at least, as far as information goes."

"It's a possibility," Lisa said, a tiny smile tugging at her lips.

"Well anyway, the first thing you should know is that Stefan is a pompous ass and something of a . . ."

"*Chitka?*" Lisa suggested.

"Definitely. Tamrovia isn't one of the richest countries in Europe, and he has these antiquated ideas about arranged marriages to benefit the monarchy. He's been trying to palm me off on every eligible royal head of state or billionaire in the world since I was sixteen. He doesn't care which as long as the power is there. Naturally I wasn't about to be manipulated, so I fought back."

"By pushing wealthy bullfighters into piles of manure?" Lisa asked with a grin.

"That was totally uninspired. Marna and I managed much more creative ways to discourage the others. Then Stefan had a brainstorm and decided that since he couldn't punish me for these little pranks, he'd go after Marna."

"Pranks?"

"The Greek shipowner developed a terrible rash," Marna said with a shrug. "Kira told him to leave her alone. I don't know what all the fuss was about. I made sure that it would go away in a day or two."

Kira's lips tightened. "Stefan put Marna in prison. He thought he could use her to pressure me."

"But you broke her out and with Clancy's help whisked her here to Sedikhan," Lisa said. Good heavens, it was like something out of a soap opera. No wonder Clancy had said that Kira and Marna were an explosive combination.

Kira nodded. "Right. That was—"

"Kira, she shouldn't be out here in this sun listening to you chatter," Marna interrupted. "I will go prepare your room, and you take her inside and get her a cool drink. Make sure she takes her iron pill with it." She turned away and walked briskly across the courtyard.

"I'm sorry." Kira looked stricken. "I didn't know you were that fragile."

"I'm not," Lisa said with a sigh. "She acts as if I'm made of glass. I had a little difficulty with the baby during my second month and she's been wrapping me in cotton wool ever since."

Kira nodded, her affectionate gaze following Marna. "She has a very loving heart, and she likes you. I can tell. She's very protective of the people she cares about."

"And I believe you are, too," Lisa said, her eyes on the girl's face.

"I love her," Kira said simply. "She raised me. My parents and Stefan never had any time for me, and Lance couldn't stand Tamrovia and was always in Sedikhan. She's been my mother, teacher, and friend." She shrugged. "Everything. That's why I can't let her be exiled like this. Marna is a gyspy and they have very close tribal ties. She hates being

away from her people. I thought maybe she'd
adjust to Sedikhan, but she's been miserably
unhappy here."

"And that's why you went back to Tamrovia?"

"What else could I do? I thought if I put up with
all that courtship bull for a while, I could talk
Stefan into a pardon for Marna." She grimaced. "I
blew it. Maybe if I'd stuck it out just a little
longer . . ."

"You're going back?"

"I can't do anything else. I have to try again." Her
shoulders shifted as if she were throwing off a bur-
den. "But that's not for a while. I'm free now and
I'm going to enjoy myself." She smiled. "Come on, I
have to get you that cool drink and your pill or
Marna will have my head."

In the hours that followed, Lisa found she was
having a wonderful time. Kira Rubinoff had the
facility of throwing herself into every situation and
relationship with a lovable enthusiasm. The girl
herself was lovable, and by the end of the evening
Lisa felt as close to her as if they'd been friends for
years.

They were having coffee in the library after dinner when Lisa first began to have a niggling sense
of uneasiness. It was almost ten o'clock. Surely
Clancy should be home by now.

"You're frowning," Kira said, eyes narrowing.
"What's wrong?"

"Nothing. I was just thinking about Clancy."
Lisa smiled with an effort. "I know you said he
might be late. I guess I worry too much."

"You worry about him. He worries about you."

Kira's expression was suddenly wistful. "It must be nice to be in love like that."

"Very nice," Lisa said softly.

She frowned. "Then why in the devil don't you marry him?" Her gaze touched on Lisa's abdomen. "You're pregnant with his child, and Clancy's too old-fashioned not to want to legitimize it as soon as possible. It's probably bothering the hell out of him."

"You think so?" Lisa asked. Clancy hadn't mentioned marriage since that night on Paradise Cay. Even then he'd assumed she wouldn't want to go through with a ceremony that would bind her to him.

"I know so," Kira said positively. "Don't you two ever talk? He's not liberated enough to embrace the concept of illegitimacy with open arms. I'm surprised he hasn't forced you before a magistrate at gunpoint."

But he wouldn't have done that, Lisa thought with a pang of tenderness. Clancy had promised her freedom, and he would never go back on his word, even if it was hurting him.

"There I go again. I know it's none of my business. I just don't like to see Clancy unhappy. Forget it."

"I won't forget it," Lisa said slowly. "Because I don't like to see Clancy unhappy, either."

And she couldn't forget about it, even after she'd left Kira and retired to her room for the night. She showered, put on a nightgown, and slipped into bed but didn't bother to turn out the bedside lamp. She knew she wouldn't be able to sleep anyway while she was worried about Clancy. Had she been too blind to notice Clancy's unhappiness with the situation? She hoped she hadn't been that self-centered, but there was a possibility that she might have been. He had seemed as content as she, but maybe . . .

The door opened suddenly and Lisa sat up in bed. Clancy! A wave of relief swept over her as she saw him standing in the doorway.

"Are you okay?" he asked as he came into the room. "I'm sorry I couldn't get back sooner, but—"

"I'm fine," she interrupted. He looked so tired. There were deep lines around his mouth, and the skin was taut over his cheekbones. "How are you? I was worried about you."

"Were you?" He came across the room and dropped on the bed beside her, then took her in his arms. "That's nice to know." He kissed her gently. "Maybe I should go away more often."

"No." Her arms tightened about him. "Oh, no."

"I brought Galbraith back with me." His hand stroked her back. "I may have to go away again for another day or two. I wanted someone here to protect you."

She stiffened. "Protect me? Why should I have to have anyone to protect me?"

"Just a precaution. I don't like leaving you alone. You're too important for me to risk." He changed the subject. "How did you and Kira get along?"

"Wonderfully. I like her very much. I'm glad she's going to stay for a while. She practically oozes vitality."

"She certainly does." He frowned. "But don't let her enthusiasm carry you away. She sometimes thinks everyone has as much energy as she does."

Lisa nodded. "I noticed that, but she's very appealing." Suddenly her eyes grew wistful. "And that gorgeous figure. I don't envy her vitality, but oh, what I'd give not to be quite so clumsy-looking."

His hand went to her abdomen and rubbed gently back and forth on the slight swelling. "It really bothers you?"

"It bothers any pregnant woman to be unattractive, even when she knows it won't last that long. There's no question that it's worth it, but yes, it does bother me." She smiled uncertainly. "Does it bother you, Clancy?"

"Unattractive?" He looked stunned. "Why the hell do you think you're unattractive? You're more beautiful now than when I first saw you."

"It's very kind of you to say that, but I know—"

"I'm not kind. I told you I'd always tell you the truth." His hands cradled her face. "Every day I look at you and see the changes and I'm filled with a kind of wonder. Your skin glows and becomes satin and velvet at the same time. Your hair shines and ripples in the sunlight. Your entire body is ripening like a young tree that blossoms in the springtime. It's all freshness and beauty and new life." He looked at her with complete sincerity. "Can't you see that?"

"No." Her eyes were bright with unshed tears. "But I'm very, *very* glad that you do." She turned her head and kissed his palm. He was the wonder. How lucky she was to have found him. "Then perhaps you won't be too embarrassed to stand up with me before a preacher."

He went still. "What?"

"I'm asking you to make an honest woman of me." She smiled shakily. "If you want to, that is. Kira said she thought you did, but if she was wrong, I'll—"

"If I *want* to!" His face had the same radiant expression she'd seen the day she'd told him of Marna's prediction about the baby. "Oh, God, *yes*, I want to." His blue eyes blazed with joy. "You know damn well I want to marry you." He suddenly frowned. "Kira didn't try to steamroll you into it, did she?"

"No, she merely pointed out that you probably wanted to make the baby legitimate. I find I want that, too." She kissed him. "I like living in sin with you, but I believe I'll love being married to you."

He drew a deep, unsteady breath. "Tomorrow. We'll fly to Marasef tomorrow and be married. I'm not taking any chances on you changing your mind."

"I'm not going to change my mind. Why didn't you tell me it was this important to you?"

"I was afraid you'd run for the hills," he said. "You were so determined not to marry after your experience with Baldwin. I didn't want to push you into giving more, when I had so much already."

"You're the one who's done all the giving." She smiled, her eyes misty. "We'll have to see if we can't change that, starting tomorrow. Now come to bed, you look terribly exhausted."

"I am." He gave her another kiss and stood up. "It's been a hellish two days. It was one blind alley after another. Every time we sent men out to raid one of the terrorists' hiding places, we'd find he'd just flown the coop. There's got to be an informer in the palace. That's one of the reasons I have to go back. I have to plug that leak." He undressed quickly, turned out the light, and slipped into bed. His arms went around her and he held her spoon fashion, his hand cupping her abdomen. "I like to hold you like this. I thought I felt a little flutter night before last. Is it time for that?"

"Yes, I've been feeling a little movement now and then."

His breathing was already deepening, his arms growing heavy around her. "Tell me the next time it happens. I want to . . ." His words trailed off, and she thought he was asleep. Then he spoke again, his voice a drowsy murmur. "So much wonder. . . ."

The tears that had been brimming suddenly ran down her cheeks. Clancy. So dear. She loved him so much in that moment, she'd thought she'd explode with it. Oh, God, and she hadn't told him that she loved him yet. She *would* tell him tomorrow after they were married. Surely fate wouldn't be so cruel as to snatch this happiness away. She didn't think she could stand it if she lost Clan— No, she mustn't be such a coward. Clancy had been all that was open and giving to her. She must be the same with him. He had lovingly taught her that a new beginning was possible for her. That beginning must be bright and brave and completely honest.

Lisa closed her eyes. She must try to sleep. She was going to be married tomorrow. But she lay there a long time before sleep claimed her, thinking about Clancy and their child and new beginnings. And Clancy's last words before he went to sleep:

"So much wonder. . . ."

Nine

The sleeveless shift was sunshine yellow in a natural silk that looked fashionable yet understated. It didn't hide the fact that she was pregnant, but it did give her a certain stylish elegance. It was the best she could do, anyway. She would really have to shop for a maternity wardrobe when she was in Marasef. Lisa turned away from the mirror. "I'm ready. It's not exactly bridal, is it?" She grinned at Clancy. "You look much more impressive than I do." He looked wonderful in his steel-gray suit. It contrasted beautifully with his golden tan and deepened the blue of his eyes. "I haven't seen you in a suit since you wore the tuxedo on the first night we arrived here."

"You look beautiful." He put his arms around her. "You're always beautiful, but this morning you have a glow."

"I'm happy." Lisa pressed a kiss on his cheek. "I think I must be old-fashioned, too. I like the idea of getting married. Will it be difficult being married in Marasef? What about all the bureaucratic paperwork?"

"Alex will fix it. I'll call him as soon as we go downstairs and tell him to arrange for a special license." He stepped back and turned her toward the door. "Let's get this show on the road."

"I'll have to tell Kira. Do you suppose she would be willing to be a witness? I don't really know anyone in Sedikhan yet, and—"

A knock sounded on the bedroom door. Clancy crossed the few remaining paces and opened it.

"Oh, you're already dressed," Kira said. "That's a relief. I didn't want to disturb you, but it's almost nine-thirty and there's still so much to do before—"

"Good morning, Kira," Clancy said with a touch of irony. "There's nothing like starting the morning with a bit of your usual zaniness. Now slow down and elucidate."

"Elucidate," Kira repeated as if she were savoring it. "I've always loved that word. Perhaps because I seldom manage to achieve the blessed state of elucidation."

"Try," Clancy suggested.

She wrinkled her nose impishly at him. "All right, but it's not nearly as much fun." She drew herself up with regal dignity. "Will Mr. Donahue and Miss Landon please have the courtesy to descend to the foyer so that we may proceed to Marasef?" She dropped the pose. "In other words, will the two of you get your asses in gear so that you don't miss this scrumptious wedding I've planned for you?"

"Wedding? But how did—" Lisa broke off. "Don't tell me; let me guess. Marna."

Kira nodded. "She woke me up at six and told me it was going to be today." She shook her head reproachfully. "You could have given me a little more time. I'm not a miracle worker, you know. I've been on the phone since seven inviting all the guests. I've called Zalandan and Philip and Pandora and . . ." She waved an all-encompassing hand. "Oh, everyone. The ceremony is set for noon at the palace with the reception directly following it." She frowned. "I would have preferred an evening reception, but I thought that would have been too strenuous a day for Lisa."

"We were just planning a simple ceremony," Lisa said faintly. She felt as if she were being swept along by a tidal wave. "I don't know. . . ."

"This will be simple," Kira assured her. "Nothing to wear you out, I promise." Her expression suddenly became grave. "It won't really be a social occasion. We just want to be there and share your happiness. Marna's tribe has a saying that to share joy is to share the soul. The only people who will be there are the people who love Clancy and want to love you." She smiled gently. "Let us share your joy, Lisa."

"You don't have to do anything you don't want to do," Clancy said. "What has been planned can be unplanned."

A very pregnant bride, a roomful of strangers who would be wondering, as Kira had, if she was good enough for Clancy. It wasn't an inviting prospect, yet these were Clancy's friends and he must want them to share this important moment in his life. It was a little thing to give, compared to what he had given her. "Why should I want to do that? It sounds wonderful." She smiled at him. "That's why you brought me to Sedikhan, remember? You wanted me to meet your people."

"Marvelous," Kira said. "Now I suggest you hurry downstairs and have your breakfast. You have twenty minutes to do that, and then I figured you could take Lisa on to Marasef in your helicopter. I've arranged for a chauffeur from the palace to meet you at the airport and take you to Alex and Sabrina. I'll follow you in the helicopter you used to fly here last night and bring Galbraith and Marna." She stopped for breath. "Okay?"

Lisa chuckled. "Okay. I have only one question."

"What? Oh, Lord, have I missed something?"

"No, I just wanted to know why you thought you weren't suited to rule a country. You obviously could reorganize the entire social structure of the world single-handed, if it suited your fancy."

Kira shook her head. "If I did, you wouldn't want to live in it. Pure chaos. Clancy will tell you." She smiled. "This is different. This is joy. I'm very good at joy." She turned away. "Now please hurry. I have to get dressed myself, and I still have to make sure the flowers are delivered on time." She was hurrying down the hall as she spoke. "I'll see you in Marasef."

"You know, I bet she *is* very good at joy," Lisa said softly as she watched Kira disappear down the corridor.

"But then so are we," Clancy said as he took her

hand. "And we're getting better all the time. Shall we go down to breakfast? We're already two minutes behind Kira's schedule. We'll have to make it up somewhere or face the consequences."

They made up the two minutes by skipping a second cup of coffee at the end of breakfast and were walking across the courtyard toward the helicopter precisely on time. Besides the familiar blue-and-white airship, there was another bright canary-yellow helicopter sitting some thirty yards distant.

"Mr. Donahue."

They turned to see Marna hurrying toward them. "I have something for you."

"Another talisman?" Clancy's brows raised quizzically.

"In a way. It's an ancient Tamrovian coin severed in two." She handed one piece to Lisa and the other to Clancy. "I have put a very powerful spell on it. If you both carry it with you during the ceremony, you will never be parted."

"That's a spell I'd be willing to try to cast myself," he said gently. He turned and opened the helicopter door. "Thank you, Marna."

Lisa impulsively leaned forward and kissed Marna's cheek. "I'll keep it always."

Clancy lifted her into the helicopter and then jumped in himself. A moment later a turn of the ignition sent the propellers whirring, and the blue-and-white helicopter lifted off with sluggish awkwardness. Then it rose, turning and gaining speed with a certain amount of grace. It made a ninety-degree turn and set course for Marasef.

Marna stood watching with a faint smile as the

helicopter sped toward the horizon. The strong sunlight glittered on the slightly unwieldy body of the craft and caused a mirror reflection on the steel fittings of the propeller. It looked terribly vulnerable and alone in the vastness of the harsh blue sky. Vulnerable. Marna's smile vanished. Her pupils dilated as the shock hit home. The airport. Vulnerable. She turned and ran across the courtyard. She had to get to Kira. *The airport.* It was going to happen at the airport!

Clancy opened the door of the helicopter and lifted Lisa to the tarmac. The shrill scream of a jet taking off on a nearby runway caused her to flinch. It was isolated at this private section of the airport, but still close enough to the main terminal to be subjected to the abrasive noise level. "This is coming as quite a culture shock. I never realized how quickly I could become accustomed to the desert quiet at the castle."

"It's only for today. By sunset I'll have you back at the castle a stodgy married lady." He grinned. "If I can manage to get you away from Honey and Sabrina and Billie. They can be very persuasive, and they're not going to be satisfied with a few hours' acquaintance. They'll be backed up by Zilah and Pandora, and I think we're going to have our work cut out for us getting away to our quiet retreat."

She frowned uncertainly. "Are you sure they'll be that eager to get to know me? You mean a great deal to them, according to Kira."

"I'm sure. Kira was right, you won't find anything intimidating about any of them." He touched her lips lightly with his index finger. "They'll love you, acushla. Trust me."

She drew a deep, shaky breath. "I will." Her sudden smile was rainbow bright. "Always."

"Always," he repeated softly. "I like the sound of that word. We'll have to go more in depth about that later." He took her elbow and turned away from the helicopter. "But right now I think I'd better get you to the palace and into the bonded state of matrimony. There's one of the palace limousines parked beside the hangar." He gestured toward a long gray Cadillac with the Sedikhan crest on the driver's door. "That must be for us. Kira will be pleased that her arrangements are going like clockwork."

"They wouldn't dare do anything else," Lisa said. "Kira and Marna are quite a combination. Together they could move mountains."

Clancy chuckled. "For God's sake, don't mention that to Marna. She might try it just to test her powers. We wouldn't want to have to reprint all the Sedikhan topographical maps. There's no telling what she's already done to the landscape of Tamrov—" He broke off, his body stiffening as if he'd been hit by a bullet. "Baldwin!"

Lisa's gaze followed him to the man who had stepped out from behind the Cadillac. He was dressed in a dark blue chauffeur's uniform with a Sedikhan emblem on the jacket pocket, the billed cap pulled down over his eyes. Oh, God, it *was* Martin! No, not when they were so happy. Not when everything was—

"Don't move, Donahue. Don't even think about

it." Martin gestured with his left hand, and she saw it contained a small, lethal-looking pistol. "We're going to take things very easy and slow. Come over here, Lisa."

"No!" Clancy took a step forward.

The gun was immediately trained on the center of Clancy's chest. "Don't think I'm not serious, Donahue," Martin said silkily. "I've waited a long time for this. I'd just as soon put a bullet in you right here."

"Don't move, Clancy. Please." Lisa pushed past him and ran across the tarmac. "You don't want to hurt him, Martin. He's a very important man here in Sedikhan. They'd never stop looking for you if you—" She stopped. She'd been about to say "killed." But she wouldn't say it. She wouldn't even think it. Nothing must happen to Clancy. "It's me you want."

"Lisa, come back here." Clancy's voice was harsh with strain.

If she could keep between them, Martin wouldn't be able to hurt him. "Let's leave now, Martin. Before they discover you're here and catch you."

"I'm touched by your concern." There was an ugly twist to Martin's lips. "I might even believe you, if I didn't remember how you tried to hand me over to your lover on Paradise Cay."

"Lisa had no part in that. The entire trap was solely my responsibility," Clancy said.

Martin's eyes wandered down Lisa's body to the slight swell of her abdomen. "I guess the kid she's carrying is solely your responsibility, too. I heard she was pregnant. We've been keeping a very close watch on both of you since you arrived in Sedikhan. I'd say both the betrayal and the kid were joint projects, Donahue."

"Martin, Clancy was only doing his job." Lisa moistened her dry lips.

But Martin wasn't listening. His eyes were narrowed with malice on Clancy's taut face. "No, I've changed my mind. The betrayal may have been a dual effort, but not the pregnancy. She used you, Donahue. Lisa is one of these women who can never love a man as much as she does a child. I found that out. She doesn't want you. She doesn't love you. She only wants that child you've put in her body."

Clancy's lips flattened to a thin line of pain. "I know that. I've accepted it. It doesn't matter."

Lisa felt a tearing agony within her. Oh, God, he really believed that! She could see it in his face. "Clancy, I—"

"Get in the car, Lisa," Martin ordered. "You drive. I'll sit beside you with this clever little toy pressed against your side and your lover will sit in the back in isolated splendor. That will give him time to think of all the very unpleasant things I'm going to do to you once we get across the border."

"Please, Martin, leave Clancy here. It will be much safer for you."

"The hell it will," Clancy said with icy menace. "If he took you and left me here, I'd cross into Said Ababa with a task force, and to hell with the border. Let's go, Baldwin."

"I had no intention of leaving you, Donahue."

Martin gestured with the pistol. "Move, Lis—What the hell!"

A canary-yellow helicopter had suddenly swooped around the side of the hangar, barely twenty feet above the ground, and was almost on top of them. The tornado stirred by the blades whipped Martin's hat from his head and sent it flying.

Lisa caught a glimpse of a flaming-auburn head in the cockpit. Kira! The helicopter dipped even lower and zeroed in on Martin's frozen figure.

"That pilot is crazy," he screamed, his eyes on the helicopter. "He's going to crash right into us!"

"Get down," Clancy muttered as he brushed by her. Then he'd reached Martin, his hand chopping down on his gun arm with lethal efficiency. Martin gave a cry of agony just as the helicopter pulled up and skimmed over their heads by a scant few feet. Another karate chop to the neck and Martin fell unconscious at Clancy's feet.

"Are you all right?" Clancy turned to her in concern. "I told you to get down, damn it."

"Everything happened too fast," Lisa said dazedly. She looked at Martin's still body sprawled on the tarmac. It had been like a nightmare where nothing was real. Except the terror. That had been very real, she thought with a shiver. "What will happen to him?"

"I decided a long time ago that when we caught him we'd send him back to the U.S. and let them deal with him." He smiled grimly. "Of course, we'll have to give them a little help. Their justice system is too lenient for my taste. I'll send an investigating team into the United States that will turn up and document every illegal act he's ever committed, every damned one of them since he was in the second grade. That will put him away for a long, long time." He frowned. "But first we'll have to interrogate him to find out who their man in the palace is, as well as where the other terrorists are located who crossed the border into Sedikhan."

"Are you all right?" Kira asked breathlessly as she skidded to a stop beside them. She was followed closely by John Galbraith. "I was terrified when I saw that horrible man with his gun trained on you as we started to land. I didn't know what to do."

"You improvised beautifully," Clancy said dryly. "Though you scared the hell out of me. I wasn't sure you were going to be able to pull up at the last minute, and I have a distinct dislike of decapitation."

"I wasn't sure she'd be able to do it, either," Galbraith said. "And she wouldn't let me at the controls."

"I didn't need any help," Kira said with a wink at Lisa. "When I was at Yale, I watched all those action TV series. The heroes were always flying around in helicopters doing things like that."

"I told you, those were stuntmen." Galbraith scowled. "You had no business—"

"You were lucky I even let you come along," Kira interrupted. "Anyone who was too thick-headed to believe Marna when she said there was danger for Clancy and Lisa at the airport doesn't deserve to be listened to."

"Marna again?" Clancy asked.

Kira nodded. "Right after you left she realized you were in danger, but she couldn't pinpoint exactly what it was. Only that it would be at the airport." She waved a scornful hand at Galbraith. "*He* wanted explanations!"

"It's a regrettable habit of mine to demand proof, instead of flying off on a whim," Galbraith said caustically.

"Well, if you'd radioed Clancy's men and had them here to protect them when they landed, instead of coming to see for yourself, I wouldn't have had to act like a stuntwoman."

"On the prediction of a gypsy soothsayer?" Galbraith asked. "What kind of professionalism is that?"

Clancy held up his hand. "John, do you suppose you could drop this fascinating debate on mysticism versus realism and get Baldwin to headquarters? We have some questioning to do."

Galbraith nodded. "I radioed for a car as soon as we landed. They should be here any minute."

Clancy turned to Kira. "I'm sorry to spoil your arrangements, but we'll have to postpone the wedding until tomorrow. We have to clear up this mess first."

"That's all right. It will give me time to do it right. Don't worry about Lisa. I'll take her to the palace and get her settled in your quarters for the night." She tilted her head, considering. "Maybe I'll call a few shops and have them send out some gowns on approval. It will give her something to do. Amy Irving was wearing the most gorgeous gown at the Academy Awards when she was expecting. It had a rich, Renaissance quality, and I think Lisa would look beautiful in something like that for the ceremony."

Clancy shook his head and turned to Lisa. "Don't let her run you ragged. Just give her a flat-out no. There are times when she even pays attention to it. Will you be all right without me? I'll join you at the palace as soon as I've wrapped this up. It's important that I find out who the informant at the palace is, or Alex and Sabrina will be in danger. You understand?"

"Of course I understand. I wouldn't have you do anything else." Lisa smiled. "Don't worry about me. I'll be fine." A dark blue car pulled around the corner and stopped beside them; the doors opened and several men emerged from the car. Galbraith immediately joined them and began issuing orders. "It seems the cavalry has arrived. Kira and I had better get out of the way and let you do your job."

"I'll have a man drive you to the palace." He leaned forward and kissed her lightly. "If you need me, just tell Alex. He'll know where to get in touch with me."

She cast a last look at Martin, who was regaining consciousness and sitting up dazedly on the tarmac. How could a man with whom she had shared so much have become such a stranger? Or perhaps he'd really been a stranger all along. They had never been able to reach each other on anything but surface levels.

"Lisa?"

Clancy's eyes were on her face, and there was something in them that reminded her of the raw pain she'd glimpsed when Martin had been taunting him. "No, it's all right," she said quickly. She couldn't bear to see that pain on his face. "You don't understand. It's not true that . . ." She trailed off. She couldn't explain here, in the midst of all this turmoil. "I'll see you later at the palace, Clancy."

Ten

"We haven't tired you, have we?" Kira asked anxiously. "I warned the others and we tried to be as careful as we could."

"No, you didn't tire me," Lisa said with a reassuring smile. "I enjoyed myself. I was glad I was able to meet everyone today before the wedding and get to know them. It will make me more at ease during the ceremony."

"I told you there was nothing to be nervous about. Now you've been officially accepted by the family." Kira looked at her wristwatch. "It's nearly eleven. I'd better get out of here and let you get some rest or Clancy will skin me." She wrinkled her nose. "I suppose I should get some sleep myself. I have to get up early to fly back to the castle and pick up Marna and bring her here for the ceremony. Our departure from the castle this morning was a little too precipitous to board passengers."

"Thank heavens it was," Lisa with with a reminiscent shiver. "I haven't even thanked you, Kira."

Kira's eyes widened in surprise. "For what? It was the best time I've had in months." She turned to the door. "Good night. I'll be here at ten in the morning to help you dress. That pink brocade gown is going to look fantastic on you." She paused as she opened the door. "Clancy called you an hour or so ago, didn't he? Is everything all right? What did he say?"

"Just that Martin had told them what they wanted to know and they were in the process of arresting not only the palace informant, but the terrorists as well. He said he'd be here as soon as he could."

"Are you sure you wouldn't like me to stay until he comes?" Kira asked. "Sometimes a strange place isn't very comfortable."

Lisa shook her head. "No, you go on to bed. This suite doesn't feel strange to me. I feel very much at home. You said I would, remember?" She smiled. "I think I'll just walk in the garden for a while and wait for Clancy. I'm too restless to go to bed."

"I can see why, after the day you've had. Well, if you change your mind, dial seven zero on the house phone. That will connect you with my suite and I'll come running. See you in the morning." The door closed behind her.

Lisa turned away and wandered over to the French doors across the room. Clancy had sounded both grim and harried on the phone. Perhaps she should wait until tomorrow to speak to him.

No! She had waited too long already. How long had Clancy been feeling that pain he had revealed today? She never wanted to see that particular expression on his face again as long as she lived. There had been too many misunderstandings, too much giving on Clancy's part, too much taking on hers. It was time to blow away all the inequalities of the past and make way for a new beginning.

She opened the French doors and stood looking out into the garden. The warm breeze touched her face and she was suddenly surrounded by scent and sound. She could dimly make out the shape of an oleander tree burdened with blossoms in the distance and suddenly heard the musical trill of a nightingale somewhere high in its branches. Or was it perched on the jasmine tree nearby?

Lisa stepped out into the soft night and closed the doors behind her. What better occupation could she find while she waited for Clancy than to go in search of a nightingale?

The private garden adjoining Clancy's suite was fantastically beautiful in the moonlight. The pale, fragrant blossoms that graced it looked like drops of moonlight themselves. White roses, camellias, creamy gardenias grew in profusion along flag-stone walkways that wound to a graceful fountain in the very center of the garden. The fountain area itself was surrounded by curving marble benches and encircled by square latticework Moorish lanterns mounted on tall, graceful spears, which glowed with the same opalescent beauty as the garden itself.

"Lisa!"

Clancy. "I'm here by the fountain."

She heard his quick, heavy footsteps, and then he appeared in the clearing beside her. "I was worried when you weren't in the suite."

"It's so lovely out here. I thought I'd wait for you by the fountain. This garden reminds me a little of the courtyard at Paradise Cay, but it's much lovelier."

"David Bradford designed this garden. He asked me what flowers I wanted planted here and I told him anything serene and beautiful." Clancy half sat, half leaned on the rim of the fountain, facing the bench where she sat. He had discarded his jacket and tie, and his white shirt was unbuttoned at the collar. "There's nothing either beautiful or serene in my line of work, and I decided they'd be very soothing." He smiled. "When I first saw you I thought of a camellia and wondered how you'd look here in my garden."

"Camellias are very fragile," Lisa said huskily. "And I'm not, Clancy. Not anymore. You've made me strong."

"You don't look very strong. That white gown makes you look like a Juliet." Suddenly he grinned. "I see Kira prevailed. Long live the Renaissance."

Lisa smiled ruefully. "Don't laugh. You may get very tired of this style. Somehow I found myself buying everything Kira suggested. She said the clothes made me look romantic, and I fell for it like a ton of bricks." She met his eyes. "Because I feel romantic, Clancy. Wonderfully, wildly, gloriously romantic."

He grew very still. "Are you trying to tell me something?"

She took a deep breath. Say the words, she told herself. "I'm trying to tell you that I love you." There, the words were out and lightning hadn't struck. Clancy was still sitting there looking at her.

His smile was gentle and a little sad. "I know that, Lisa. I know you feel something for me or you would never marry me, no matter how grateful you are. I saw how upset you were when Baldwin was taking those little jabs at me, but you didn't have to do this. What I told Baldwin was true. I've accepted the fact that you can't love me as I love you. It doesn't matter to me."

Struck speechless for a moment, she stared at him. Then she burst out, "The hell it doesn't!" She jumped to her feet, her eyes blazing. "I know damn well it means a hell of a lot to you, just as it would to me if I didn't believe you loved me. Yet you're sitting there looking at me as if I were a half-wit child who's not responsible for her own actions."

"Lisa . . ." Clancy stood up, a startled expression on his face. "I didn't mean—"

"I know exactly what you meant to do. Protect Lisa. Care for Lisa. Love Lisa. Well, isn't it time Lisa gave some of that back?" She took a step nearer, her hands clenched into fists at her sides. "I am *not* a camellia. I am *not* a princess in a tower. I am *not* an emotional cripple incapable of love. I'm a person of reasonable intelligence and immense emotional potential. And all of that emotional potential has been tapped by you, Clancy Donahue. I *love* you. And it's not the puny, insipid affection which is the only thing you seem to believe I'm capable of. It's big and it's deep enough to fill my entire life." She drew a quivering breath. "And so strong that it scares me silly when I think of you crossing a street or when I see you fly away in the helicopter or just run down a flight of stairs." Her voice dropped to just above a whisper. "Because I survived what happened to Tommy, but I'm not at all sure I could live without you, Clancy."

He shut his eyes, his body tense. "For God's sake, don't tell me that if you don't mean it, Lisa. I've grown accustomed to the idea that you could never give me—"

Her hands went to his shoulders and she gave him a little shake that was far from gentle. "Open your eyes and look at me, dammit. What does it take to get through to you?"

Obediently he opened his eyes and she saw a glimmering of radiance in their depths. "I think you're beginning to succeed." His chuckle was a little husky. "Maybe if you tried a karate chop or two." He picked her up and swung her in a wild, boisterous circle with a joyous laugh. "You mean it? Oh, God, you really mean it?"

"I don't know karate." She was laughing, too, her eyes alight with the same joy. "But I could learn. Because I'm not—"

"A camellia," he finished for her. "Or a princess, or—" He broke off to kiss her with an exuberance that flooded her with happiness. He lifted his head. "But you are my love and the mother of my child and the center of my particular universe. Will you accept that, acushla?"

"Oh, yes, I'll accept that." She nestled her head against his shoulder. "Gladly."

He picked her up and sat down on the marble bench, cradling her in his arms. "I think we'll dispense with the karate lessons until after the baby is born. I think you're being put through enough daily turmoil without that." He placed one hand gently on her abdomen. "I was worried about you after that mess at the airport this morning."

"You shouldn't have been. The baby evidently thrives on excitement. He's been very active this afternoon."

"Really?" His other hand joined the first, splaying out gently, searchingly. After a moment his eyes flew to meet her own. "I'm not jealous, you know," he said. "I want you to realize that. I couldn't be. I already love our child very much."

"I know," she said softly, and felt an aching tenderness tighten her throat. "It wasn't true what Martin said, Clancy. Perhaps it might have been in Martin's case because I never knew what love was all about then. I've been thinking about that while I sat here waiting for you." Her arms tightened around him. "There are all kinds of love in the world. Mother for child, friend for friend, lover for lover. All separate but equal." Her head nestled in the hollow of his shoulder. "Then, sometimes, if we're very lucky, we're given a love that's very special and combines all of those in one. That's what I feel for you, Clancy. It doesn't mean that I loved Tommy or will love our child more or less than I do you. There's no way of comparing love, because it's all joy." She was silent for a moment, searching for words. "Remember that gypsy saying Kira told us about? To share joy is to share the soul. Well, to share love does the same thing, Clancy. It goes into every part of our minds and hearts and binds us together so that there are no shadings, no comparisons, nothing but one shining entity." She closed her eyes and her voice was a mere breath of sound. "Isn't that wonderful?"

"Wonderful," he echoed. He swallowed and then laughed huskily. "Lord, I feel like I want to shout or cry or . . ." He shook his head. "I don't know . . . something. I didn't think this could happen to me. I thought I'd missed the boat somewhere along the way. It took such a long time coming." His lips pressed gently against her temple. "But now I've got it all. After half a lifetime of waiting, it's really here."

"*We've* got it all," she corrected softly. "And who knows, if it had happened earlier, we may not have been ready for it. Maybe we needed to grow to this point so that we could fully appreciate what we have. I know I probably did." Her eyes opened to gaze at him with love. "You've had such a rough day. Do you want to go inside and go to bed?"

He shook his head. "I don't feel tired. I feel young and strong and so damn happy that I want to wave banners and send up flares. I couldn't sleep if I tried. I just want to sit here and hold you." His big hands moved gently on the swell of her stomach. "And maybe feel our child move beneath my hands. Could we do that?"

The tears were brimming, but Lisa refused to let

them fall. This was not a night for tears, not even tears of joy. "Oh, yes, love, we can do that."

She closed her eyes again and relaxed against his warm strength. It was quiet and fragrant here in the garden, and they were surrounded by peace and delight and love. So much love. Now was the time of serenity and anticipation. There was really no need to do anything at all but listen to the sweet song of the nightingale in the oleander tree and wait for the stir of new life to come.

THE EDITOR'S CORNER

As you know from the sneak previews I've been giving in the Editor's Corner, you have some wonderful treats in store—and none better than the four for next month!

We start off with a gloriously intense and touching love story in **CHAR'S WEBB,** LOVESWEPT #151, by Kathleen Downes. The story begins on an astonishing note: Hero Keith Webb has "invented" a fiancée because the young daughter of a friend has a crush on him and he wants to let her down gently. For his lady love he had chosen a first name he'd always liked, Charlotte, and for her last—well, his imagination failed and he had only come up with Smith. Now, just put yourself in Keith's place when the management consulting firm he hired sends out one of their best and brightest employees and *she* introduces herself as—you guessed it!—Charlotte Smith. The real Charlotte is as lovely, sensitive, and tender-hearted as Keith's fantasy fiancée . . . but she's also devoted to her job, has vowed never to mix work and love and—ah, but to say more would give away too much of a vastly entertaining and twisty plot, so I'll only encourage you to anticipate being trapped like Keith in the enchantment of **CHAR'S WEBB.**

If you've just finished **ALWAYS,** my guess is that you feel as though you've been wrung out emotionally. (I certainly felt that way when I read and worked on that marvelous love story!) Now, for next month, Iris Johansen greatly changes pace with **EVERLASTING,** LOVESWEPT #152, in which she gives you a romp of a romance. Oh, it is intensely emotional, too, of course, but it *is* also a true "Johansen romp." You met Kira Rubinoff in **ALWAYS** and may have leaped to the correct conclusion that she was your next heroine. In **EVERLASTING** she is off to America for help to rescue her beloved Marna . . . and

continued

that help is in the form of one Zack Damon, powerful industrialist, famed lover, part American Indian and proud of his heritage—in short, just one heck of a hero. Now for the romp part: there are gypsies and dungeons, palaces, plots, magic, and kings. And there is grand, glorious, passionate romantic love between Kira and Zack. Iris simply keeps coming up with one lovely romance after another, and aren't we lucky?

Our other two authors for the month—the much loved Miz Pickart and Miz Brown—have just as wonderful and fertile imaginations. First, you'll enjoy Joan's charming **MISTER LONELYHEARTS,** LOVESWEPT #153. The title refers to the hero's occupation: he writes a newspaper advice column, focusing primarily on love and romance. Heroine Chapel Barclay is a lawyer—and a lady who is as mad as a wet hen at the "Dear Ben" column and the blasted man who writes it! She thinks the advice he gives out is garbage, pure and simple, that it's destructive to creating real and lasting relationships. When they confront one another on a television talk show, Ben is the overwhelming winner of their debate . . . and later full of remorse that the lovely Chapel had suffered from his remarks, even though he'd softened them because of her remarkable effect on him. But if Ben and Chapel had thought sparks had flown between them on that telecast, did they have a surprise ahead. When he sought her out to apologize, it was the beginning of a physical and emotional conflagration that made the great Chicago blaze look like a small campfire! Another memorable winner from Joan Elliott Pickart.

Sandra Brown's stunningly beautiful contribution to your reading enjoyment next month is **22 INDIGO PLACE,** LOVESWEPT #154. A romance of conflict and drama and sensuality, **22 INDIGO PLACE** is aptly titled, since the house at this address has played such an important role throughout the lives of the heroine and hero that it

continued

almost becomes a living, vivid character in the story. And the story of James Paden and Laura Nolan is breathtaking. James was the high school "bad boy"—complete with motorcycle, black leather jacket, and shades. Laura was "Miss Goody Two-Shoes." Their contacts back then were brief yet fierce, and when they meet again their impact on one another is just as dramatic. But now, added to James's devastating sensual power over Laura, is his economic power. How he wields it and witholds it makes for one of Sandra Brown's best ever love stories.

We hope you enjoy these four LOVESWEPTs as much as everyone here in the office did.

Warm good wishes,

Sincerely,

Carolyn Nichols

Carolyn Nichols
  Editor
LOVESWEPT
Bantam Books, Inc.
666 Fifth Avenue
New York, NY 10103

Hi! Do you remember I told you Clancy's story was going to be the last in the Sedikhan series? I swear I fully intended it to be true, but as I was writing Always a character popped up needing her own story. Now what kind of author would I be if I hadn't given in and written it for her? That's how Everlasting was born. My vow turned out to be half true anyway, because Everlasting is more a story about close kin than about Sedikhan. Sedikhan and Tamrovia, where Everlasting is set, are what you might call sister countries, though. I hope you enjoy both books, because while I was writing Everlasting a certain character began to intrigue me and. . .but that's another story.

I'm still working part-time at an airline, and my children, Roy and Tamara, are still in college. They have been traveling extensively on their school breaks. They've visited San Francisco, Las Vegas, New York, Honolulu, Nassau, and London. They fell in love with London and all things English, and want to return as soon as possible. I may decide to go with them. The atmosphere and ambience of that lovely city is a positive magnet.

Thank you for your cards and letters. Your support means a great deal to me. Have a wonderful summer. Be happy.

LOVESWEPT

LOVESWEPT® · 148

IRIS JOHANSEN
Always

It began as a daring, desperate scenario to flush out a
terrorist, a man whose crimes were serious enough for
Sedikhan security chief Clancy Donahue to kidnap a
stunning American singer to act as bait. A man who'd
never known any true lover but danger, Clancy had no
defenses against the beautiful captive whose spirit and
passion imprisoned his heart. Lisa vowed to resist the
flames of need that burned in her blood, but soon both
were consumed by an aching desire that was as
overwhelming as the merciless desert sun. Before he
could offer his beloved all the rest of his days, though,
Clancy would be forced to risk her life....

LOVESWEPT

*Love stories you'll never forget,
by authors you'll always remember.*

Australia *$2.50
New Zealand *$3.50
        *Recommended Price Only

21749

0 76783 00250

N 0-553-21749-6>>250